HURRICANE

Also by Terry Trueman

URRICANE
A NOVEL

TERRY TRUEMAN

HarperCollinsPublishers

For Jesse Cruz Trueman

Library of Congress Cataloging-in-Publication Data
Trueman, Terry.
Hurricane : A novel / by Terry Trueman.—1st American ed.
p. cm.
"Previously published in the UK under the title 'Swallowing the Sun' . . .
story and characters have been completely revised and rewritten for
this US edition"—T.p. verso.
Summary: A fictional account of one of the worst storms to hit the
Caribbean—Hurricane Mitch in 1998—told from the perspective of a
thirteen-year-old boy living in a small village in Honduras.
ISBN 978-0-06-000018-9 (trade bdg.)
ISBN 978-0-06-000019-6 (lib. bdg.)
1. Hurricane Mitch, 1998—Honduras—Juvenile fiction. [1. Hurricane
Mitch, 1998—Fiction. 2. Hurricanes—Fiction. 3. Survival—Fiction.
4. Honduras—Fiction.] I. Title.
PZ7.T7813Hu 2008   2007002990
[Fic]—dc22   CIP
                                                                      AC

Typography by Larissa Lawrynenko
09 10 11 12 13 CG/RRDB 10 9 8 7 6 5 4

First American Edition
This book was previously published in the U.K. under the title
Swallowing the Sun. However, the story and characters have been
completely revised and rewritten for this U.S. edition.

ACKNOWLEDGMENTS

First and foremost I'd like to thank Toni Markiet, again, for her brilliance as an editor and friend (I told you this book could be done, Doc!!). *Hurricane* appeared in a different form/version, quite different really, at Hodder Books in the UK under the title *Swallowing the Sun* (2001), and Beverley Birch was the editor, so I'd like to thank all the people at both HarperCollins Children's Books and Hodder for their help with the story. Thanks to George Nicholson, my agent and a prince of a guy, and to his assistants at Sterling Lord Literistic, Inc. Thanks to my wife, Patti, and my son Jesse, to whom this book is dedicated. Thanks also to my many friends from so long ago in Honduras, especially Ginger Ninde and Reza and Marlee Khastou. I must acknowledge my "reader" friends who dedicate many hours of attention to "works in progress," helping me to make those works better. Finally, thanks to the usual suspects: writers, pals, librarians, teachers, Sheehan, and everyone else who has made this career of mine possible.

LA RUPA, HONDURAS

MARCH 1998

It's early on a Saturday morning in our little town of La Rupa. I'm in a championship soccer game on the main street of town—actually the *only* street in town. Today this street has become a soccer field. All our neighbors are out cheering me on. They smile and wave and jump up and down. Even my dog, Berti, looks interested, and nothing ever gets her very excited. But one voice stands out from all the others. "José," a man with a deep voice says. "JOSÉ!" the man calls again. But when I open my eyes, the soccer field and all my adoring fans are gone.

My older brother, Víctor, wakes me up with a gentle tug on my shoulder. "Come on!" Víctor says, giving me the "shush" sign so that I won't wake our little brother, Juan, sleeping in his bed across the room. Berti wakes up too, lifting her head and staring at us. She gets up to follow.

Víctor leads me to the back door before I even have any breakfast.

I'm grumpy, but Víctor ignores my mood. When he has a plan, like he has right now, there is no changing his mind. I can tell by the look in his eyes that he is on a mission.

It is a nice morning. The air feels warm and a little damp. Our grass is chopped really short because Ernesto, the man who cuts it for us with his machete, was here just a few days ago. I glance up at the hillside behind our house, behind all the houses on this side of La Rupa. Last year a logging company cleared lots of the trees off that hill. The trees used to be home to the wild parrots that fly overhead on most days. The parrots are still around, though; they just moved a little bit deeper into the forest.

Víctor interrupts my daydreaming. "Look at this," he says, nodding at the huge, dirty, old brick barbecue that has stood just outside our back door since we moved into this house. Both Berti and I stare at it.

Víctor smiles and says, "This thing has got to go."

I ask—stupidly, I'll admit, but after all it's still early in the morning, "Where's it going?"

Víctor laughs. "We have to tear it down and get rid of it."

I look at it again, tall and brick and sturdy. "Why?"

Víctor says, "Mom and Dad have their twenty-year wedding anniversary coming up. Mom has never liked this thing, and it's ugly. Dad suggested that we could tear it down and make the backyard nicer for their big celebration."

Our mom likes to cook outside, since the days and evenings are warm and humid. She uses a small barbecue we have in the back, but she has never used this big one. None of us have ever used it, and no one in La Rupa has anything like it. Still, looking at what Víctor is suggesting, I can see that it's going to take a lot of hard work.

Víctor and Dad are probably right. Tearing the stupid thing down is a good idea, but it's going to get hot today, like it does every day, and it isn't going to be easy to break all these bricks apart.

"Víctor," I say, "this is going to be a pain."

Víctor looks at me and smiles. "José, anything worth doing is usually a pain, but getting rid of this thing will make our home nicer. Think of how much better our house will look when your preppy friends from your rich kids' school come to visit. It'll be great. Come on, just help me for a little while. Let's get to work, okay?"

Víctor often teases me about my "preppy friends." I think he's always been a little jealous of my going to the International School, where we're taught in both Spanish and English. He calls me "preppy" when he wants to give me a hard time. He doesn't understand that I kind of like this nickname because I like being called the same thing that all the rich kids at school are called. Who knows? Maybe someday I'll be rich too! Víctor didn't go to a bilingual school. When he was starting school, Dad's business was just getting going and our family couldn't afford the high tuition then. Besides, Víctor had always wanted to work with Dad anyway; school was never important to him. I'm the student in our family, not my big brother. He's a hard worker, though, strong and tough and stubborn like Dad, only different. In ways it seems like Víctor is almost a grown-up already. He's always been almost a grown-up. I don't know how else to describe it. I'm not going to say that Víctor is kind of bull-headed, but that doesn't mean it's not true!

So for now, like it or not, I'm a worker too, and Víctor's helper.

I look over at Berti. She's lying in the sun, relaxed and comfortable. She doesn't know how lucky she is to be a dog. In all the many months we've had her, she's only learned one trick: sit. When you roll a ball for her, she just looks at it. When you call her to come to you, she only does it if you have a treat in your hand that she can smell. Playing, running, and even taking a walk are of little interest to her. Berti's idea of an exciting life is to lie around all day doing . . . well . . . nothing.

I have no such luck today.

Mr. Arroyo, who lives with his wife behind their little store across the street, is already sweeping his porch like he does every morning. He's a funny, smart, nice guy. When he glances in our direction, he smiles and waves. The kind of "store" he and his wife have is called a *trucha*. Most neighborhoods and most small towns in Honduras have them. I've seen movies from the United States where they have Circle Ks and 7-Elevens, small stores where you can buy a few things when you need them. Here in Honduras we have truchas that are built in the front part of people's houses. The only trucha in La Rupa is at the Arroyos'.

In the first half hour of tearing the barbecue down, a crowd of neighbors gathers along the street and the side of our backyard. It starts with the kids, but eventually parents come over too. We have a big audience. The Arroyos lean out the window of their little store and smile, and Vera Ramírez, who lives next door, cooks bacon and eggs in a skillet over a little fire in her backyard while watching us. Eventually almost all of La Rupa show up: the Handels, Mr. Marpales, the Cortez boys, Mr. Ramírez, the Ortegas, the Baronases, the Altunezes, Mr. and Mrs. Cortez, the Barabons, and the Larioses. Everyone wanders by to watch us for a while. Truth is, there are not a lot of other things to do in town anyway.

"Hey, Víctor, that's quite a structure to be tearing down," says Mr. Ramírez, smiling, "only I'm not sure what La Rupa is going to do without our jailhouse."

Víctor laughs.

I whisper to Víctor, "Jailhouse?"

Víctor smiles at me and says quietly, "He's just kidding, but look at this thing—built of bricks and almost big enough to be a jail."

I pick up a load of bricks and stack them against the back fence, where Víctor has told me to put them. When he first suggested this idea of storing the bricks, I asked, "Why are we saving them, Víctor?"

He looked at me like I had asked the stupidest question in the world. "These bricks aren't cheap. What do you want to do, just throw them in the street?"

"No," I answered, but I couldn't think of anything else to suggest.

Víctor patiently said, "We'll find a use for them someday, José. Maybe Dad and I will pave the patio area, or maybe we'll find someone who wants to buy them, and we can haul them out of here then."

I said, "Oh, sure. That sounds good."

"For now, though," Víctor said, "let's get them out of the way and stack them neatly against the back fence there, okay?"

I tried to think of some argument against moving them all that way, but I just answered, "Okay."

So hauling bricks is my job, and as we work, I make a bunch of these trips.

Allegra Barabon calls to me, "José!" I glance over and see her twirling one of her pigtails around her finger. "Do you feel like a mule?" I don't answer, but I force myself to smile at her dumb joke.

Our sister Ruby, who is sixteen and the unofficial beauty queen of the town, comes out and watches us too. Ruby says teasingly, "My goodness, Víctor, you are truly the greatest brick barbecue destroyer in all of Honduras."

She looks over at our crowd of neighbors and smiles. Now she says to Víctor, "As you can see, such talent does not go unrecognized nor unappreciated!"

Our neighbors smile back at Ruby, and Víctor laughs again.

A little later, Ruby brings us glasses of lemonade. I sip mine slowly. Víctor inhales his in one gulp.

Dad comes out of the house and sees all our neighbors standing around. He goes over and visits for a while with Mr. Marpales and Mr. Cortez. When Dad walks by us to go back inside, he says, "Excellent, Víctor. What an improvement tearing down this monstrosity will be."

Víctor smiles and seems very proud. But when Dad sees that Víctor isn't looking, he winks at me.

I try to pretend this horrible task isn't really happening. I see the flock of wild parrots, soaring overhead. They're so graceful. I look up at the steep hill that rises along the north side of town just behind our house. This hillside is a green wall that protects us from the world. The loggers clear-cut part of the hill, but I still love the forest even though it's no longer so close to our home.

I smell the smoke of breakfast fires around town, especially from next door, where Vera Ramírez has finished cooking. She looks over at me and gives me a thumbs-up sign. I manage to smile back despite how miserable I feel. I've known Vera Ramírez since I was born. She's like a second mom to me.

Some of the kids, led by Carlos and Pablo Altunez, tire of watching us and go out in the street to play soccer. I wish I could join them.

As I carry bricks, I see all the houses of our little town. Glancing at our neighbors who stand talking together, I realize that I know every home in La Rupa and the colors, shapes, and sizes of every room in every home. The houses here are just like most houses in Honduras—simple buildings, with one bathroom and two or three bedrooms. We don't have basements like I've seen in movies about the United States, or big two-car garages. But our houses are painted more colorfully, in bright pink or yellow or turquoise. I have been inside all these houses many times, eaten meals with the families, and watched TV with the kids. I know where the picture of Jesus, with his chest open and his heart showing, hangs on the living room wall of the Hernández house; I know that the Álvarezes always have pink toilet paper in their bathroom to match the pink tiles on their bathroom wall. I know exactly where the canned hams or canned peaches are in the Arroyos' trucha. I know every person in every home, where they sleep, where they eat, and who gets along or doesn't get along with whom.

The only family that I don't know really well, a family no one in town knows very well, is the Rodríguezes, squatters who live on the opposite side of town from our house, poor people with three kids and no money. They moved here a few months ago. Their "house" is made of tarps, two-by-fours, and scraps of weathered plywood. Every neighborhood and small town in Honduras has at least one Rodríguez family. Nobody minds them being here. They are just poor people who have no place else to go. But we haven't gotten to know them very well either, because these families move often, never staying in any one town or neighborhood very long.

After an hour and a half of working, Víctor and I have the barbecue torn only about halfway down. Víctor is being very careful to not break the bricks as he uses Dad's wrecking bar and a hammer to pry them loose and then sets them gently on the ground.

I stare at the Altunez and Cortez boys still playing soccer in the street. They've been joined by Jorge Hernández, who is my age, and Félix Marpales, who is a year older but a small guy and not very athletic. If I were playing, I'd be the best soccer player in the group. I *so* wish that I could join them!

"Go ahead, José," Víctor suddenly says, nodding his head toward the street.

I ask, "Really?"

Víctor says, "You've helped a lot. Go play soccer. I can finish this up."

I look at the rest of the barbecue still standing, and I want to say that I'll stay and help, but I can't make myself say it. Instead I ask, "Are you sure?" knowing that Víctor will say yes.

Víctor smiles. "Yeah, go."

I feel guilty, but I can't stop myself. "Thanks," I say as I take off toward the street. "See you."

"See you too." Víctor immediately gets back to work.

Berti sees me moving toward the street and slowly, lazily stands up and starts to follow me, but she only walks ten or so steps before she stops. I look back at her and ask, "You wanna play soccer?"

She sighs a dog sigh and plops back down onto the ground in a spot where she can watch both Víctor working and me playing. Berti might just be the laziest dog ever born. Teasing her, I say, "You can be goalie," but she drops her head onto her paws and looks back at Víctor again. "Suit yourself," I say, running to join the game.

I score six goals in our marathon match. I am the star . . . at least to myself!

* * *

Five hours after we started, Víctor is finally almost finished. The news spreads throughout the town, and soon all our neighbors—most everyone in La Rupa— comes back to watch Víctor complete the job. Our soccer game breaks up for good, and all of us go to watch too. As we approach the yard, Berti gets up again and trots over to stand near me.

When Víctor has unloaded and stacked the last of the bricks, he walks back toward the house and says, "That's it."

Many of the adults burst into applause. They call out, teasing, "Bravo!" "Encore!"

Angelina Altunez, Carlos and Pablo's mom, says, "You are a great man, Víctor."

Víctor won't let our neighbors see him blush, but he smiles, raises his arms, and takes a dramatic bow, which makes everyone laugh, cheer, and applaud even louder.

My shirt is soaked with sweat just like Víctor's, only mine is from playing soccer for the last three hours, and now I feel guilty that I didn't help Víctor more. I also have to admit that I feel a little bit jealous that Víctor is getting all the credit, even though he deserves it. If I had known that Víctor would become La Rupa's hero and main attraction for the day, maybe I would have kept helping. Then again, maybe I wouldn't have. Víctor is the oldest. It's his job to do things like tear down huge, ugly barbecues. I'm only thirteen; my job is to help him a little bit and then go have fun.

I glance at Víctor as he finishes his bow. To tell the truth, I'm hoping that he'll say something like "José helped too," but he just smiles at me. As much as I hate to admit it, Víctor really did do most of the work. I guess fair is fair.

Berti looks up at me and kind of smiles in that way that dogs do when they seem calm and happy. I reach down to pet her, but she licks the soccer-game sweat off the palm of my hand before I can start patting her head. Víctor may be La Rupa's hero for the moment, but Berti still likes me best—at least right now she does.

As I look around at all our friends and neighbors, I can't imagine La Rupa ever changing very much. We're a tiny Honduran town in the middle of nowhere. Towns like ours are not just in Honduras or even just Central America. They can be found anyplace, really. Then again, what do I know? I've lived here all my life.

SIX MONTHS LATER

ONE

"Berti! Come! Come on, girl!" I'm standing on our front steps, yelling down the street and then in the other direction, over and over again. Berti never wanders away for very long, but she hasn't been home for several hours.

"BERTI! BERTI!"

Mom opens the front door and says, "That's enough, José. She'll come home when she gets hungry."

"But Mom . . ." I start to say, but she interrupts me.

"You're too loud, son. Come in and have dinner, and after you eat, you can go look for her some more."

I say, "Okay," but I'm not really happy about it.
Where is that stupid dog?

It's not just Berti who is missing dinner. There are only five of us home tonight. It's been rainy all day, a hard rain (the kind of rain that Berti *never* goes out in!). Víctor and Ruby are with Dad on his deliveries. Dad delivers goods—everything from expensive furniture for rich people's houses to groceries for the little truchas in the small towns near here and in the closest big town, San Pedro Sula, seventeen miles away. Dad is almost always home in time for dinner, but tonight he's late. I figure that the storm must have slowed him down. Víctor works with Dad on most days, and Ruby had to talk to some people at a modeling school in La Ceiba, seventy miles away, where Dad's deliveries are today, so she rode along with them.

Mom decided not to hold the meal any longer, which I'm glad about, because I'm hungry!

I ask my sister María to pass me a tortilla. This sounds like a poem because María rhymes with tortilla. Anyway, I ask her a second time, "Hey, María, will you pass a tortilla?" I get sort of a kick out of myself. María either ignores me or doesn't hear me. With her you can never tell. She's always got her head in the clouds. Why doesn't she do a poem back at me, something funny, like "No way, José. I must say, you'll get no tortilla from María!"?

"María," I ask again, louder, "will you please pass me a—"

I don't finish my sentence because in this instant the rain and wind hit our roof with a huge pounding sound—a noise like thunder or something big and heavy ramming into the house. It hurts my ears. Our house shakes under the weight of this noise, and there is a bad creaking sound, as if the boards will give way and collapse. I feel a shiver run up my back and get goose bumps on my arms, as if I were watching a scary movie. I try not to let anyone see me looking scared.

But as I'm thinking this, my mother, who was walking toward the table from across the kitchen when the noise hit, freezes in her tracks, standing as still as a statue. Juan and my youngest sister, Ángela, both stare up at the ceiling.

María looks at me and asks, "What?" She is the only person in our house who has not noticed how bad the weather has suddenly gotten.

"Shush,'" I say to her quickly, holding my finger up to my lips. Juan and Ángela stare at me, and in another moment even María looks nervous.

"*Mamá,*" Juan calls out, and Mom hurries over and wraps her arms around him. I wish Mom were holding me right now, even though I'm too old.

It bugs me that I'm scared of a stupid storm. I tell myself that it's only rain and wind, just water falling down from the sky. But the truth is I *am* scared. This is so different from any rain we've ever had. During the rainy season, we have lots of storms. Many times during sudden cloudbursts I've ducked into the house and watched the rain pour down. But there's never been anything like this rain before. It's not even like rain; it's more like sheets of solid water, like a waterfall crashing down from the sky. And the wind gets worse and worse, roaring all around us. What a stupid time for Berti to go missing!

Where are my father and Víctor and Ruby? Why aren't they home yet? Mom wasn't too worried earlier, because it *is* the rainy season and Dad is used to driving in bad weather, but this is beginning to feel like something much worse than just a regular storm.

The water shifts its weight; the roof creaks again. Rain now drips down into the house, and it is a *lot* of water. On the rainiest, wettest days of past rainy seasons, sometimes our house leaked in one or two different spots, a place in the kitchen and a place just over the back door. Now the house has sprung too many leaks to count. Mom, Ángela, and María hurry to grab buckets, pots, and pans—anything to catch the dripping rain. I can't tell where one leak ends and another begins. The water drips into the house so fast and steady that in some places it looks like it's coming from a faucet.

"José," Mom calls to me, "grab some black garbage bags and cover up the TV and stereo." As I grab the bags, the rain that leaks from the roof drips down onto my head and neck. It's cold and feels awful. I use duct tape to hold the corners of the bags down. And when no one is watching, I throw a bag over Berti's sleeping blanket, lying at the foot of my bed. She'll be wet and shivering when she gets back, and a dry place to sleep is the least I can do.

Mom puts plastic over the clothes that hang in our closets, and now we find some large plastic tarps and lay them over our beds to try to keep our blankets from getting too wet. Already a lot of our stuff looks like it's ruined. Ángela's favorite doll, Juanita, is on the floor in the living room, soaked. It looks like a drowned baby. I try not to look at it; it's too creepy.

Realizing that I've been more worried about stupid Berti than about my family, I think about Dad again, and Víctor and Ruby. Are they all right? When will they get home? I feel cold and scared even here in our house; what must they be feeling, caught in this weather? Tears come to my eyes a little bit as I think this. My fingers and hands feel cold too. I'm wet and uncomfortable, but worst of all I'm ashamed of being so afraid. The rain pounds and pounds, and the wind blows harder than ever. Where are my father, brother, and sister? Where's my dumb dog? What's going on?

Ángela, having run out of containers to catch the dripping rain coming through our roof, flops down on the couch, picks up her drowned doll, and begins to cry. María sits cuddling Juan, and Mom is still trying to catch the water. There's a gnawing feeling in my gut, my chest aches, and my palms are tingly and damp, not just from the rain. I've never felt this scared before.

TWO

We had known for a few days, from the news on TV, that Hurricane Mitch was coming toward Honduras. But no hurricane has ever really bothered us here in La Rupa before. We're not close enough to the shore, and in the past, by the time a storm's winds and rain came this far inland, it wasn't a big deal. This time Dad had even promised Mom that he'd beat the weather home, but when he said it, it was like a joke. Nobody's laughing now.

Another strange thing about Berti being gone is that I haven't heard any of the other dogs in town barking for a while, not for hours and hours. Normally the dogs bark a lot. Berti isn't a barker at all, but the others are always pretty noisy. This evening, though, they are silent. I wonder if they've run away too.

The TV is not working. In fact, all the lights went out a little while ago. We listen to María's little battery-operated radio and learn that this storm, Hurricane Mitch, is different from any of the others that have come before. They call it a Category 5, the worst there is, with winds and rain unlike any we've ever had before.

Except for the rain, it was calm and quiet here right up until the moment that the wind really started pounding us. For the last hour, both the rain and the wind have gotten worse and worse.

Ángela says, "I'm afraid, Mom."

"I know, Angie," Mom says. "Try not to worry too much. We're all here with you."

I fake a laugh. "It's just rain and wind; it's no big deal."

María says, "It's a *hurricane*, brainiac! Don't tease her for being afraid of it."

"I just mean that we're safe here," I say. "Everything will be okay."

Ángela says, "What about Daddy and Víctor and Ruby?"

None of us says anything, but as I think about her words, I get a sick feeling in my stomach.

Mom stares at the floor. Then she looks up and answers, "I'm sure Daddy and the others will be fine, but say a few prayers just to be sure, okay?"

"Yes, Mom," Ángela says. María nods.

Juan doesn't say anything. He just stares at the front door, like if he stares long enough, Dad and Víctor and Ruby will walk into the house. Seeing him like this makes my stomach feel even worse.

I go to my bedroom and put on my warmest jacket and hurry back out into the living room.

Mom asks, "Where do you think you're going?"

I say, "To find Berti. You said I could after dinner."

Mom asks, shocked, "In this weather?"

I answer as I start to open the door, "It's not that bad. It's just—" A huge gust blasts me in the face. The raindrops feel like small stones. I lean into the wind and try to move forward, but another gust pushes against me hard and actually throws me back half a step.

Mom says, "Berti is probably somewhere safe, waiting out the storm. That's what you should do too. You're not going to find her in this weather."

A third big gust pelts my face with raindrops and shoves me back into the house, convincing me that Mom is right.

"Okay," I say, closing the door.

I didn't even go outside, but the front of my jacket is sopping wet and my face is red and stinging from the rain. "Maybe I'll try again later, when the wind calms down," I say.

"Good idea," Mom says.

I strip off my jacket, which is completely dry in the back, and hang it on a kitchen chair. I grab the dish towel from the front of the stove where it hangs and wipe the dripping water off my face.

For another hour we sit. We talk a little, but mostly we're quiet so we can listen to María's radio. Candles light the living room, and we move chairs and the couch around to avoid the dripping rain from our ceiling.

Two or three times I think I hear Berti at the door, and I get up to go let her in, but every time it's just the wind tossing debris against the house.

Finally Mom says, "It's getting late. We need to try to get some sleep."

I blurt out, "How are we supposed to sleep through this noise?"

Mom looks at me, and I can see how worried she is. I take the hint and say, "Sorry, Mom. You're right. We should get to bed . . . sorry."

Mom smiles at me. Maybe she hopes that if we just go to bed, when we wake up all this will be over. She's just scared like we are. I see fear in her eyes and in the way her forehead is wrinkled with worry. But I agree with her—we may as well go to bed. Why just sit here in our dripping house, staring at each other? I'm worried about Dad and Víctor and Ruby, though, and I can't stop my hands from shaking every time I think about them. I'll bet Mom is even more worried than I am.

I consider trying to find Berti one more time, but the wind is howling just like it was earlier. Mom's probably right: Berti is hiding somewhere, maybe in one of our neighbors' houses. She'll probably come home in the morning. Yeah, I'm sure—once everything quiets down, she'll find her way home.

In the bedroom I share with my two brothers, Víctor's empty bed is covered with plastic. In the soft glow of the candle we brought in, I can see Juan. He lies silent in his bed with a scared look that never leaves his face. Once we are in our beds, with plastic tarps covering us over the tops of our blankets, I blow out the candle.

Juan's been quiet ever since the storm started. He's usually a chatterbox, carrying on and on about everything and everyone. Although my little brother is only four years old, he watches every music video that comes on and knows all the words. He can read the backs of cereal boxes and understand what's written there. He even speaks pretty good English, because my sisters and I talk to him in that language and because he goes to a bilingual preschool three days a week. Juan's got a collection of plastic action figures that I'm sure rivals any collection in the whole country of Honduras. He has Víctor's old ones and all of mine too. He has at least a couple of hundred.

They make up a weird group of characters and scenes. It's funny to see Juan playing war games with an old Teenage Mutant Ninja Turtle and an equally old Luke Skywalker. Sometimes Juan has a baseball player doing mortal combat with Simba from a *Lion King* Happy Meal. He loves to play with these toys in bed at night too, but tonight, in the wet cold of our room, Juan's very quiet.

I ask him, "Are you afraid, Juan?"

"No," he answers, very softly.

"I'm scared," I say.

"Really?" Juan asks, his voice a little shaky. "Why?"

"Oh, I don't know. I just am. This rain and wind

is so loud, you know?"

"Yeah," Juan answers. I can almost hear the wheels turning in his head. "I won't tell Víctor that you're scared," he says.

I smile and say, "Thanks, Juan. You're a good brother."

Juan and I are quiet for a few moments until he says, still very softly, "I'm a little bit . . ." He won't let himself actually say the words.

"That's okay," I say. Then I add, "I won't tell Víctor either."

Víctor is a good big brother, but I know why Juan thinks we should keep our fears to ourselves. Víctor is very macho. He thinks crying is for sissies, and he's not the kind of guy who would ever admit he's afraid of anything. And while Víctor is almost always kind to Juan and me, he does have a temper.

One day last year I walked out of the Baskin-Robbins ice cream store in San Pedro Sula. I had ridden into town with Víctor and Dad just to hang out in the big city. Two Anglo kids a couple of years older than me were standing nearby. They weren't students at my school, and I didn't know them. The taller kid wore a baseball cap.

I stood there with my double-scoop chocolate waffle cone, minding my own business. It was the spot where I was supposed to meet Víctor.

Out of the blue, the kid in the cap turned toward me and said, "Hey, Sánchez, I didn't think you guys ate anything but beans and rice."

His friend laughed and said to his pal, "You'd better talk slower. He maybe doesn't speaka da Engleesh too *bueno*, ya know?"

They both laughed.

The first kid asked in a very thick, exaggerated Spanish accent, "Hey, 'scuse me, *señor*, you likey American icey-creamo?"

They both laughed again, but the one who'd just spoken stopped laughing pretty fast when suddenly his head jerked to the side and his Arizona Diamondbacks baseball cap flew off his head.

I hadn't noticed Víctor come up behind them. After slapping that first kid, he grabbed the other kid by his shirtfront and said in a low and mean voice, speaking mostly in English, which Víctor almost never does, "You like Frito Bandito jokes too, *pendejo*?"

The kid stared at Víctor and answered in a scared, shaky voice, "No."

I said to Víctor in Spanish, "Take it easy, they were just—" But he interrupted, his expression very angry.

"Shut up!" he snapped.

He grabbed the kid whose hat he'd knocked off by

his shirtfront too and, holding both of them, asked him in Spanish, "*¿Tienes preguntas?*"

They looked really scared.

I said, "I hope you can understand my English okay." They both looked surprised. "My brother is asking if you have any questions."

Neither of them said a word, but they both shook their heads.

Although they were as tall as Víctor, they were probably fourteen years old. Víctor was sixteen then. Víctor isn't that big, but he is pretty muscular. He has black hair and very dark eyes and skin. I don't know what it is, but something seems to always make people stand back and respect him.

Víctor stared back and forth between them for a few moments more, as if he were daring either of them to say anything at all. Finally he gave them both a hard shove, and they flew backward. He turned to me and said, "Are we ready? Let's go."

As Víctor and I left, I looked back. One kid walked over, watching us nervously the whole time, and picked up his baseball cap. Then they both hurried away.

Víctor turned to me and said in Spanish, "Listen, José, I think sometimes you feel that guys like them and the rich gringos like the kids at your school are better than us, but some of them have no respect.

They aren't better." He paused a second and smiled. "Did you see their faces?"

I smiled too; I couldn't help it. "Yeah . . . they looked pretty nervous."

We both laughed.

Víctor said, "We keep this to ourselves, okay? Dad wouldn't like what I did."

I answered, "Sure, Víctor."

Two seconds later we both laughed when Víctor said, "You speaka da Engleesh pretty *bueno*, *amigo*!" and punched me in the arm.

Now, in the dark bedroom, Juan interrupts my thoughts. He says, "Catch," just as I hear a *splat* on the wet plastic tarp that covers my blankets.

I reach around the top of the tarp until my fingers find what Juan's thrown. It's his C-3PO action figure, the gold android from *Star Wars*.

Víctor had the entire *Star Wars* collection when he was little. Juan lost Princess Leia and threw away Jabba the Hutt because Jabba was too scary. He still has all the others. C-3PO is his favorite.

"Are you sure you want to lend me this?" I ask.

He says softly, "Yes."

The wind suddenly howls even louder and the rain pounds down. I say, "I'll give him back to you first thing in the morning, okay?"

"Okay," Juan answers, but he still sounds really scared.

"You can have him back right now if you want. I mean, I know he's one of your best ones. You sure you don't want him back?"

Juan is quiet for a few seconds and then says, "You're kind of scared too. You can use him tonight."

"Thanks, Juan."

"Okay," Juan answers back.

In another few minutes, I hear Juan snoring softly, just like he snores every night. His snores sound funny, so tiny and weak. I probably should have given him C-3PO back, but maybe he feels good thinking he's helping me.

Talking to Juan and comforting him let me forget about my own fear for a few minutes, but now it's back, worse than ever.

I glance at the big green digital numbers on the battery-operated clock across the room next to Víctor's bed: 10:08. This storm has been going for four hours now without slowing down at all.

How long can it keep going?

I don't know when exactly I finally doze off. Maybe some of the time I'm asleep, I'm dreaming I'm still awake. But finally I do have a dream that I know, even while it's happening, is a dream. It's Christmastime in La Rupa. Never do five seconds pass without the sound of firecrackers popping. Sparkling bottle rockets and whirling flames fill the daytime sky. The blue smoke and the smell of gunpowder fill the air. I feel like I might explode with happiness. This Christmas Day is just like every Christmas I've ever known. The smells, the sights, the warm feeling on my skin—everything is perfect and wonderful.

Suddenly, I see a flock of beautiful wild parrots fly across our backyard, their black eyes staring at me. Their stares feel strange, though, like they are trying to warn me of some danger.

Now back in my house, I try to open a present, only it's wrapped too tightly. I tug and pick away at the wrapper, but I don't seem to be getting anywhere. I hear a terrible low growling sound. I look up from the gift. The growl is too deep and scary to be a dog, even a large dog. Suddenly Berti stands next to me. Staring in the direction of the horrible sound, she growls back, showing her fangs, wanting to protect me. The sound slowly turns into a soft, frightening howl. I am scared, but I don't want to show it. Maybe by acting brave, I will be all right. The gift in my hand turns into a large gray stone, a weapon I can use to fight off whatever is howling just outside the walls.

I wake up. There's a little bit of rainwater puddled on the tarp, right over my lap. For half a second I'm embarrassed because it looks like I've wet my bed. Now I'm wide-awake, hearing the storm howling. I look over at Juan's bed, where he's awake too.

The rain has stopped. Maybe when we get up, the sun will be back and everything will be normal.

"Are you awake?" Juan asks.

I answer, "Yeah."

Juan quickly asks, "Do you think it will rain again?"

I answer, "Maybe, but probably not so heavy and not for so long."

The wind is still blowing hard, but without the rain it doesn't feel as scary.

Juan says, "I'll bet Víctor is mad at the rain."

"Oh yeah," I agree. "Víctor is probably telling the rain just what he'll do to it if it starts falling down on us again."

"Yeah," Juan says. "Víctor will kill the rain if it keeps falling."

I smile and answer, "He will, Juan. He'll kick the rain's butt!"

Juan loves to hear Víctor and me talk like this. He's

scared that he'll get in trouble if he says these kinds of things, but I can always make him smile or giggle when I talk a little bit bad.

"I'll bet Ruby's sad and worried about us," Juan says.

I answer, "I'm sure she misses you. But she'll be home soon, and then she'll give you a big hug."

"No way," Juan says. "Yuck!"

I smile. Juan wouldn't want Víctor to see him enjoying a hug from Ruby. Víctor would call him Baby-J, a nickname Juan hates.

Juan's quiet for a few moments. Then he asks, "They are coming back, huh?" His voice sounds very tiny. "They love us, even when we're bad, so they will come home, right?"

Could Juan think that Dad and Víctor and Ruby are gone because of him, because of some bad thing he thinks he did or thought? Little kids are so weird.

I am quiet for a bit, trying to think how to make him understand.

"Juan," I say, "the storm has kept them away. It's not *your* fault. This storm has nothing to do with us, with how good or bad we are. *Everybody* is getting rained on, good guys and bad guys both. It's not our fault. It's nobody's fault. Dad and Víctor and Ruby will be back when the storm stops. And it *will* go away someday."

"Yes," Juan says. I can hear the sleepiness in his voice, and sure enough, within a few minutes I hear his little snores again.

I lie in the darkness thinking about what I've just said to Juan. The storm will go away—if only I could believe this myself!

I glance over at Víctor's clock again. 12:18.

Before I can fall back asleep, the rain comes back, but it's not like the rain from earlier. It's not so heavy, and the sound of it falling is almost nice, like rain is supposed to be. The winds have calmed down too. I feel safe for the first time all night. My hands are steady and my insides are calm. My breathing feels almost relaxed. Maybe the storm *is* over.

I start to think about Berti again. How stupid and selfish can I be? She's just a dog, for crying out loud, and not much of a dog at that. But with the storm calmer now, I'm not as worried about Dad and Víctor and Ruby as I was earlier, so Berti comes back into my thoughts.

I remember when I first met her. She showed up in La Rupa about a year ago. I was out in the street by myself kicking a soccer ball, when suddenly this medium-sized tan dog came trotting right up to me. I saw her coming from way down the street. She never hesitated as she walked, with her head up and her eyes looking straight at me. She stopped about ten feet away from me and barked.

I said, "Hi." She walked right over to our house and just sat there at the foot of our steps, looking back and forth between the house and me. Her ears stood up and she wagged her tail. It was almost like she felt that our house was her house, and like she was waiting for me to invite her in.

I went over and petted her on her head and back. She was muscular and had short hair. She smiled as I scratched her neck. After a while I went up the steps and walked into the house. The dog followed me as if she'd done it a million times before.

She hung around the house the rest of the day. I noticed that she had a black tongue. It was a little pink but mostly black. I worried that she had the plague or something, but when Dad came home, he explained that she was probably part Shar-Pei, a breed of dog from China, the kind you see in pictures with too much wrinkly skin.

"Shar-Peis have black tongues," Dad said. "Yep, she must be part Shar-Pei and part shepherd or collie, which would be the part where her smarts come from."

Everybody in the house oohed and aahed over the dog all night. She licked everybody's hands and kept wagging her tail.

Dad said that when he was a boy, he had a great dog. "This new dog is so sweet and relaxed that she reminds me of Roberto," he said. Dad started calling her Roberta, and pretty soon she became Berti.

At school the next day I looked up Shar-Pei in an encyclopedia. Under the part where they say what the breed is supposed to do, like German shepherds are good guard and search dogs, Jack Russell terriers are rat killers, collies herd, and Labradors hunt, Shar-Peis, I learned, have been bred over the centuries for . . . nothing. Under the category for Special Talents was just that one word: *nothing*. And sure enough, Berti has been pretty much true to her Shar-Pei bloodline: good at almost nothing except being sweet and happy and laid back.

So where are you tonight, Berti? Out in this storm? When are you coming home? Why did you run away?

I've always thought of Berti as *my* dog, partly because I found her and let her into the house that first day, and partly because I just *want* her to be mine. Víctor works with Dad every day, so he and Dad are best friends. Juan is the baby and gets most of Mom's and everyone else's attention all the time. My sisters aren't into playing with a dog, so Berti should be mine. But the fact is that Berti is nice to *everybody*. Every kid in our house thinks that Berti likes him or her best. Whoever gives Berti a bite of a burrito or tortilla is definitely her favorite human at that moment.

Yet I'm the guy who has to take all the responsibility for her. I always have to feed her. I also have to clean up her messes in the yard, which is gross. This was the deal when my parents agreed to let us keep her.

I'm tired of thinking about this. Berti is gone now, but like Mom said, she'll be home when she gets hungry. The heck with her. I don't even care if she comes back or not.

Well, that's not really true.

I finally fall asleep again.

I dream that I'm flying over Honduras, only it doesn't look like Honduras. There are bright lights, like fireflies, only brighter. I soon recognize that the lights are coming from the little houses of La Rupa below me. Two wild parrots are flying next to me. One of them is so close that I can see his eye. It is bright and shiny and looks right back at me. It feels good to be so free.

Suddenly there is a tremendous explosion, like the world is cracking in two. All the lights below me go out, and I can't tell if I am flying or falling in the darkness. The wild parrots disappear. I hear a strange, distant sound of crying and moaning. In the darkness, just waking up from my dream, I am confused. The earth quivers under my bed.

Juan cries out, "José!"

I jump out of bed and grab Juan into my arms.

The house seems to shake all around me.

Is it really shaking, or is it just my legs?

Is *any* of this real?

Before I can get my bearings, there is a huge *THUMP!* and now I know that it's not just me. It's like a bomb went off.

I stumble into the living room, still carrying Juan. Mom and the girls are here too. We have all managed to find one another in the dark.

Mom asks with panic in her voice, "What is it? Is anyone hurt?"

I answer, "Juan and I are okay."

"I'm all right," Ángela says, "but it's like the world is breaking apart!"

"I'm okay," María says.

Mom says, her voice firm, "Nothing is breaking apart . . . we have to stay calm."

I make my way to the window and look out. There is a river of mud surrounding the house and covering the street as far as I can see in the darkness.

I yell, "It's a mudslide!"

"Oh God," Mom says.

I stare out the window again, looking as hard as I can. "The mud isn't moving anymore. It's stopped!"

Mom says, "Everyone stay calm." She shines a small flashlight on each of us. Juan, dressed in *X Files* underpants and a white T-shirt, reaches out to Mom, and she grabs him from me.

Now voices outside are calling out for help. They grow louder and louder.

"Is that Dad and Ruby?" Juan asks in a tiny voice.

"No," I tell him. "It's our friends—our neighbors."

I hurry back to my room and pull on my pants and a T-shirt. I grab my jacket and slip into my Nike high-tops.

By the time I come out of my bedroom, Mom is standing at the front door with a larger flashlight. She hands it to me and says, "Be careful!"

I look into her eyes, and I can tell how scared she is. I'm sure that she wants to tell me not to go out, but we both know that I have to. It's what Dad would do and what Víctor would do too. My hands shake and my stomach flip-flops. For a second I just stand there, hoping Mom will tell me I can't go.

But she squeezes my hand and says, "Be careful, José!"

"I will, Mom. I promise!"

I open the door and step outside.

THREE

It's just drizzling now, but it's still dark as I get ready to move off our front porch. My flashlight is useless, a tiny dot of light that doesn't even reach the houses across the street, much less farther away. I stand still for a moment and keep passing the light all around the town. I don't see anything, but I hear people crying out. I move toward their voices.

I take two steps off our front porch and sink into the mud. I scream out, scared that it will suck me all the way down, but the mud comes up to only my knees. My heart pounds and I am frozen for a second.

I take some deep breaths before finally struggling

to push through the mud again. I manage to move one foot and then the other, slow and hard, slogging as if I'm moving in slow motion.

I keep waving my flashlight so that the people calling can see and yell over to me and I can find them, but this stupid light is so weak! Where are all the houses? Where are . . . And now it hits me. The Ramírez house, which used to stand right next door to ours, is mostly *gone*.

I force myself to look into the darkness, squinting as hard as I can trying to find the other houses, but I can't see *anything*. I don't know what time it is, but it must be nearly sunrise, because as each second passes, I can see farther and farther down the street.

Oh my God!

It's not just the Ramírez house that is gone; so are the Arroyo and Álvarez houses and the Larioses' house and . . . All the houses are gone!

All I can see is a river of mud. Far on the other side of the village there is a sudden fire. Flames rise up for a few moments and then they fade away.

This can't be real, can it?

If all the houses are gone, where are all the people?

Where are the people who were sleeping in those houses?

Where *is* everyone?

All the voices I heard calling for help a few moments

ago are suddenly quiet. There's a terrible silence.

But now I hear moans coming from where the Ramírez house used to be. I try to hurry there, but I move too slowly through the mud. The roof has been torn off their house and lies in the street, flattened out. The walls of the house are buried, and only the tops stick up. Mud is everywhere, brown, wet, and thick. It looks like the filthy fur of an animal.

Where are Mr. and Mrs. Ramírez?

Only a few days ago Vera Ramírez smiled at me and waved. I waved back. It was quiet that day, calm and relaxed, with only a warm breeze. Suddenly I see Mr. Ramírez. He is sticking up out of the ground. His hair is matted down with mud. His eyes dart around as he whips his head back and forth. I try to reach him, but I can barely move.

I look down and can't see my feet. The mud covers my ankles. How many times have I kicked a soccer ball on this street, the street that is gone now. How many times have I run past the Ramírez house or the Álvarez house—or all the houses—heading home after school?

Mr. Ramírez's cries jar me. At first, I can't make out what he's saying, but now I hear him more clearly.

"Vera!" he calls over and over again. For a crazy second an image pops into my head of Vera and my mom making tortillas or fried bread together.

"Vera!" Mr. Ramírez calls again.

I call back to him, "I don't see her!"

"Vera?" he yells to me.

"No, Mr. Ramírez. It's me, José Cruz."

"Where is Vera?" he moans.

"I don't see her," I yell again, finally reaching him. I am close enough to grab his wrist. His skin is freezing cold, and his bony arm feels like it could snap in my hand.

I ask, "Can you move your legs? Are you hurt?"

"Don't worry . . . about . . . me. Find Vera!" Mr. Ramírez gasps. His voice sounds raspy and weak, and while he tries to talk, he keeps stopping to get his breath.

I fight back tears and force myself to think of something to say. "I . . . I don't know where she is, Mr. Ramírez. I . . . I don't see her. Let me help you first. Then we can both look for her. I . . ." No more words will come.

But Mr. Ramírez understands and answers, "Yes. Good, José." He looks up at my face as I get closer. His eyes are filled with tears.

I move behind him and reach under his arms and across his chest, locking my hands. His body feels so cold. Once I have him in a strong grip, I begin to tug him up. At first I sink in deeper, and I'm scared that the mud will swallow both of us. But in another few seconds Mr. Ramírez begins to break loose. Just as Mr. Ramírez is getting free, Carlos and Pablo Altunez come from where the street used to be. They fight their way through the mud toward me.

The sky is light now, and we can see everything, but there is nothing left to see.

In all of La Rupa, only two whole houses still stand—our place and, way across town, unbelievably, the Rodríguez family's tiny shack, which the mud didn't reach. These two places, the Rodríguezes' and ours, are the farthest apart of all the houses in town. When the mudslide came down, it came right through the middle of La Rupa, wiping out everything between our two places. Parts of some houses still stand, but they lean at terrible angles, held up only by the mud, three and four and five feet deep, packed around them. All that's left of most of the houses are broken rooftops lying on the ground.

Carlos and Pablo ask, "Can you help us? Our parents are buried. Help us, please!"

Pablo begins to cry.

"Vera is lost," Mr. Ramírez says. "Vera! Vera!" he calls out.

Pablo, crying harder, begins to moan, "My God, My God!"

I stand helpless; if only my dad or brother were here. They'd know what to do. Suddenly I hear myself saying to Carlos and Pablo, "Go back to your house and dig! Hurry! Use a shovel if you can find one, or a stick, or your bare hands if you have to. Maybe your parents are still alive. Go and dig them out!"

Carlos and Pablo move back to where their home used to be. They go as fast as the mud lets them.

Mr. Ramírez begins to dig, using his bare hands, calling out, "Vera! Vera!" over and over.

"Let me help," I say, pushing my hands into the mud and pulling out handful after handful. But after a few minutes I hear the groans and cries of other people again—other people who need help too. I leave, making my way toward the other voices. Mr. Ramírez doesn't seem to even notice that I'm gone.

I move through La Rupa, toward the broken, leaning houses and past the rooftops lying on the mud. I don't know which way to turn. Where is Víctor? Where's my father? They'd know what to do. My eyes start to burn, but I hold back the tears. I take deep breaths and force myself along what used to be the main street of town but is now just an ugly river of mud. My legs and feet feel like they're being scraped raw with sandpaper, but I have to keep moving. I have to try to help.

FOUR

Mr. Ramírez sits on a mud-splattered chair in front of where his house used to be. His mouth is twisted tight, and his eyes are dark and red. He looks sad and confused. I walk past him on my way back to my house, looking at him quickly but then looking away. Vera Ramírez lies on the ground next to where Mr. Ramírez sits. She is dead. I can't bear to look.

I'm so tired that I can hardly stand up, much less walk.

After trying to help Mr. Ramírez and then the Cortez family, I went to all the other places where houses used to be. After hours and hours of digging,

I am finally back home.

Mom hugs me and says, "Are you all right?"

Tears come to my eyes, so I look down at the floor. "Yeah."

Mom asks, "How are the others? Who have you found?"

Still fighting back tears, I answer, "Thirty-two people are probably dead. Vera Ramírez, too . . . so thirty-three in all. Thirty-three of our . . ." My feelings overwhelm me and I can't say any more. I stare at the floor.

Shocked, Mom says, "From our town of fifty-six, thirty-three are—"

I answer before I can stop myself, "Dead! They are all . . . dead. They . . ." I just can't talk.

Mom begins to cry but quickly wipes her tears away and says, keeping her voice low, "We have to stay strong, José, for your brother and sisters."

Brother? She says this like I only have one brother. Thinking about Dad and Víctor and Ruby again, I ask Mom, "Where *are* they?"

Mom answers, "I sent them all back to their rooms to try and get more sleep. They're all exhausted."

Mom is telling me where the younger kids are, not answering my question. But I let it go. If she knew where they were, she'd tell me. It was stupid of me to ask.

It feels like we *all* have died. The faces of the people who are gone now keep racing through my head: Mrs. Ramírez and all the times she was there just to talk with me and laugh at my stupid jokes; Allegra Barabon with her hair in pigtails and the gap between her top two front teeth; Raúl Ortega kicking a soccer ball; the entire Hernández and Marpales families; Mr. Baronas, who walked kind of funny ("bowlegged," Dad called it); and Mrs. Handel, who always smiled about everything, and her two children, Julio and Margarita—all of them . . . all of them . . .

I can't do this . . . I can't stand it . . .

My eyes start to sting with tears again. I force myself to think of other things, stupid things, soccer, *carne asada*, my school, Berti lying in the sun . . . but gone now too . . . I try to think of anything other than my friends, buried in the mud—buried alive. . . .

I sit on the floor in the corner of the living room. My body aches, and my legs and arms feel weak. I don't want to cry, but I'm so worn out.

Mom asks, "Do you need some water or something to eat?"

But I am not thirsty or hungry. "Not right now," I say.

Mom says, "José, you've done great. Stay strong, son."

I nod. If I try to talk, my voice will crack.

Before last night, there were twelve houses in La Rupa, and except for going to school in San Pedro Sula, this little pueblo was my whole world. Before last night, there were twelve families living in those houses. This place was home. Now we are gone!

Mom convinces me to go to my room and try and get some rest. I tell her that I'm all right, but to make her feel better I go.

Juan snores in his bed.

I'm asleep before my head even hits my pillow.

When I wake up and walk out into the living room, I am surprised. Nine or ten people sit quietly, listening to María's radio, which tells us that all over Honduras it's just like here in La Rupa. People say that misery loves company, but I don't think that the news about this storm's damage makes anyone feel better.

Ángela says to Mom, "How can this happen to us?"

María answers Ángela. "It's happened to everyone, not just us." Both girls glance at our neighbors. Some are on chairs or the couch, but most of them are on the tile floor. Almost everyone here has lost at least one family member, and most have lost more than one.

"I know." Ángela begins to speak to María. "But

how . . . ?" Her voice breaks and she starts to cry.

María puts her arm over Ángela's shoulder and hugs her close.

Juan doesn't say anything, but it's like he's glued to Mom. She quietly rocks him on her lap.

No one talks much.

We just listen to the news, and it seems like all of it is bad.

No one talks. What is there for any of us to say?

My friend Alfredo Mendoza suddenly walks into town and up to our front door. Alfredo lives with his family just outside La Rupa. Thinking about all our lost homes and people here, I forgot about the Mendozas because they are not really part of the pueblo. They have a farm about a half mile away, through the trees and over a small hill.

To call Alfredo my friend isn't really true. Like me, he goes to one of the two private bilingual schools in San Pedro Sula; but his school is the International Sampedrano, my school's archrival. He plays soccer on his school's team. He and I are the same age and have competed in soccer ever since we were little. Now, though, none of this matters at all. I am just glad to see him and happy that he is okay.

I ask, "Is the rest of your family all right?"

He nods.

"What . . ." Alfredo begins to ask. Then he finishes his question. "What happened to all the houses?"

"Mudslide," I say.

Alfredo is silent for a moment.

Now he speaks to me in English so that our neighbors won't know that he's talking about them. "What are you going to do with these too many people?"

I glance at everyone. Some are injured, and some are so tired and sad that we can't tell if they are hurt or not.

I just shrug and answer back, also in English, "I don't know, Alfredo. The only other house still standing is the Rodríguez place. It's very small, but they've taken in neighbors too. They have ten people there."

"Ten people?" Alfredo asks.

I nod.

Neither Alfredo nor I have to say what we are both thinking: How can ten people even fit into the Rodríguez shack? There is only one room in their whole house for the five of them. It's a miracle that the wind and rain didn't tear the place apart and just pure luck that the mudslide didn't reach them.

A few of the people sitting and lying on the floor listen to Alfredo and me and start to look nervous. They probably wonder why we're speaking in

English, what we're hiding from them.

I shift our conversation back to Spanish so that everyone will understand. "We will help everyone we can for as long as we can. My father and older brother and sister are . . ." My voice starts to quiver. I pause a moment and take a deep breath. "They are missing." I fight as hard as I can to sound calm. "We haven't heard from them since the storm started."

"I'm sorry," Alfredo says quietly.

But I barely hear him, because it hits me that I've just said that Dad and Víctor and Ruby are missing. The radio has told us that thousands of people are missing. A sick feeling rises in my stomach.

"Not missing," I say quickly. "We just haven't heard from them yet."

"Sure," Alfredo says.

There's a long, awkward silence between us.

Finally I ask, "Can you take some people back to your house?"

Alfredo looks around at everyone packed into our living room. Some of them look up at him and some of them intentionally look away. "I'll ask my mother," he says, and then quickly adds, "I'm sure she'll want to help."

"Thank you," I say.

Mom walks over and smiles at Alfredo. She pats

his shoulder and says, "Yes, thanks." Alfredo smiles back at her and nods.

Mom asks Alfredo, "You and José are soccer friends, no?"

He smiles some more, glancing at me, and says, "More like soccer enemies, maybe."

I smile back and say, "Not anymore."

Mom says to Alfredo, "Tell your mother that I said hello, that we are all together in this, and that I will visit her in a few days."

"With pleasure," Alfredo answers Mom.

As he leaves, Alfredo promises that he'll be back before dark.

Once Alfredo is gone, everyone falls silent again. It's eerie because at this time of day La Rupa is usually so noisy. What do you call a place that's still here but isn't really, a place that just yesterday was full of neighbors and houses and wild parrots and kids on Big Wheels?

If I close my eyes, I can see the town exactly like it was, all the houses still here and all the people still alive.

And now there are only three real houses: ours, the Rodríguezes', and, just a little ways away, the Mendoza place, not a part of La Rupa before but a part of us now. I look closer at my friends and neighbors sitting with me: Carlos and Pablo Altunez, wearing filthy, mud-covered pajamas and mud-caked athletic shoes; Mr. Larios, fully dressed but not wearing shoes; and many others barefoot too, and coated or splattered in mud. Everyone sits staring at the floor or into space, silent, like ghosts. La Rupa isn't gone, but I don't know what it is.

When I first started to learn English, I found that there isn't one word that means both the people of a place and the place itself. In Spanish *pueblo* means "people" and "village," and sometimes it even means "country." There's just one word for all of that.

La Rupa, our pueblo, *has* to survive, because if it dies, my dad and brother and sister won't have any place to come back to.

La Rupa is not gone, not as long as any of us are still here.

FIVE

In our backyard I get my first real look at the hill-side. The mud came down right where the trees were clear-cut last year. Like I said before, our house is at the farthest edge of town, like the Rodríguez house, which just happened to be a few feet away from where the mud flowed. Our house was mostly missed by the mudslide too. What destroyed all the other houses would have taken us down too if we hadn't been lucky. Why were we spared? Why was our house just out of the path of the mudslide? I wish there were a reason, but there isn't one, nothing except dumb luck.

There is an enormous boulder five or six feet from the back door of our house that was left by the mudslide. It must weigh tons. The bottom half of the boulder is covered in mud, but the top half was cleaned by the rain. It's almost as tall as I am. It wasn't there before.

I look at our backyard and see the spot where Víctor and I stacked all the bricks the day he took down the old barbecue. Now those bricks are all over the yard, thrown around by the mud and knocked aside by this huge rock as if they were just tiny pebbles.

I walk over to the corner of our backyard, mud up to my ankles. I stare out at what used to be La Rupa.

For the first time since this all started, because no one is nearby, and especially because my brother Víctor is not here, I cry. I cry hard, letting everything out. My chest hurts and my ribs ache. My nose runs. I cry and cry, and as bad as it feels, it also feels good. It feels right to cry like this. Weird thoughts race through my brain: All my life I've been afraid of being weak, afraid even to let myself cry. As I weep now, though, I feel different. I'm not ashamed, not embarrassed. Tears stream down my cheeks and find their way into my mouth. These tears have a gritty taste to them. Crunchy tears, I think. In another moment I am laughing and crying at the same time. Finally I can't cry anymore. I wipe my arm across my nose and rub my eyes with the heels of my hands to get rid of the last of my tears.

I've spent my whole life looking up to Víctor and my dad, but they aren't here. Dad and Víctor can't help us. It's up to me now. I know what I have to do and I can—I *will*—somehow do it.

SIX

The radio announcer says, "The storm is over."

Over?

Ha!

Just the fact that the winds and rains have stopped doesn't mean that anything is over. And here in La Rupa nothing is over. Everything is just starting. We have no drinking water at all, and no running water. We have no working toilets, no telephones and no electricity, and we are all alone.

The battery-operated radio says that all across Honduras, and in Nicaragua, Costa Rica, parts of Guatemala, and even all the way to El Salvador, thousands of people are dead.

But he also says that tens of thousands are missing.

Missing.

Like Dad and Víctor and Ruby.

The radio tells us:

The airport at San Pedro Sula is under three feet of water. . . .

Out in Xalopa some people have been sitting on their roofs for more than thirty hours without water, food, or help, trapped. . . .

The beaches of Tela and Sula, where Dad used to take us to swim and hunt lobster and play in the sand, are completely destroyed. . . .

The Bay Islands, Honduras's greatest and most beautiful place, have been wiped clean. Not a single building still stands. . . .

What will happen now to our country and our people? Will we ever recover from this? Will we ever be happy again? We are almost gone now. As I think about my dad and Víctor and Ruby, and even about poor Berti, my mouth gets dry and I feel sick. There is something worse than gone, and that is not knowing, maybe *never* knowing, where your loved ones are.

What could be worse than gone?

Never knowing. . . .

SEVEN

"I know this sounds terrible and I'm so sorry to have to say it, but we must leave the rest of the bodies where they are," Mr. Cortez says, tears choking off his words.

For two days now the men of La Rupa and we older boys—Pablo, Carlos, Enrique Larios, Jorge Álvarez, Alberto, and I—have dug and scraped at the earth, searching for survivors. Using shovels and rakes, sticks, and our bare hands, we've clawed our way into the mud, hoping and praying that we will find more of our neighbors, family, and friends. Our hands are bloody with blisters, cuts, and scratches.

My back aches from so much digging. But we've found no one alive and only the dead bodies of one child, Edgar Barabon, and one adult, Rosa Handel.

In our living room, a dozen people sit crammed together, deciding what to do about the people who are still buried. Everybody agrees that by now, two days and nights after the mudslide, no one is still alive down there.

Suddenly Mr. Ramírez mumbles, "I pulled my Vera out, and now she is wrapped in plastic, under stones in the yard." He pauses, staring off into space. Dirt still covers his body. His fingers are cut and torn from using his bare hands to dig. He seems so different now, not like the same man who only a week ago gave our soccer ball back to us with a two-handed, over-the-head toss like a sideline throw, or who, a few months ago, teased Víctor about tearing down our barbecue jailhouse.

Mr. Cortez looks at Mr. Ramírez sadly, and then he looks around the room at all of us. "Perhaps later we will be able to bring everyone up from the mud— maybe when we get help. But right now we have no coffins, we have no place to put the bodies—and we can't help those who are already gone."

There's silence in the room, but we all nod. It's not just Mr. Ramírez who has changed. I barely recognize these people, my neighbors whom I've seen every day for my whole life. How long will it be until help arrives? If all of Honduras is as bad as La Rupa, what if no help ever comes?

Even though the hurricane is over, a steady rain falls all afternoon. But the worst of the storm has passed. What more can happen to us now anyway? How could things be worse? As I think this, I remember Dad, and Víctor and Ruby. Things could be *much* worse. My stomach aches and churns.

Mom brings in two large pots, one of beans and one of rice, cooked in boiled rain water, and sets them on the table in the kitchen. There's no tap water to wash the dishes, but nobody complains about having to use a slightly greasy plate or fork or spoon. Everyone comes to the table to dish up. The kids go first, and even the younger ones know not to take too much food. Nobody pushes or shoves. Nobody asks for more than their share or argues or complains about the portions they're served. Everyone just says, "Thanks."

Looking at my neighbors and friends, I feel proud of us all.

As I'm finishing my meal, Mom says, "José," and signals with a tilt of her head for me to follow her.

I set my plate down and go. As we walk out the

back door, I look at the huge boulder, thinking again how lucky we were that it stopped rolling when it did. I've set up Mom's small barbecue near the big boulder. Our stack of firewood is wet, but with enough newspaper we easily got a fire going.

Mom shuts the door behind us. I see the worry in her eyes. I'm surprised to see Mom like this. She's been so strong. I think about the way she's held Juan, the way she spoke to Alfredo, and how she has made all our neighbors feel so comforted and welcome. To see her scared now makes me afraid too.

"Look," Mom says, opening the black plastic garbage bags that hold our supplies of beans and rice.

I'm shocked by how little is left. I ask, "How can there be so little food?"

Mom answers, "There are just so many of us."

She's right. She's cooked servings for ten people for two days now.

Mom's next words jar me. "We *have* to find more food, *fast!*"

I say, "But all the houses are buried."

Mom nods and stares at the ground for a moment.

I say, "Maybe I could walk to San Pedro Sula and bring back what we need."

Even as I say this, I know it's a stupid plan. San Pedro Sula might as well be a million miles away with all this mud and the flooding we've heard about on María's radio.

Mom says, "San Pedro is too far."

"I know. Maybe help will come. Maybe . . ." I feel so stupid. If Dad and Víctor were here, what would they do? I can't think of any good ideas at all!

Trying to keep the worry out of my voice, I ask, "Where will we find food?"

"Maybe the Arroyos'?" Mom says gently and a little bit guiltily.

Of course! The Arroyos' little grocery! Their trucha had lots of canned goods—milk, beans, baby food, fruit, vegetables, meat, tuna—lots of stuff.

I ask, "How can we get it?"

Mom says, "You'll have to dig. The Arroyos would have been the first to help us if . . ." She hesitates.

I know that she is right, and I agree with her. "I'll dig."

EIGHT

The first thing this morning, the third day after the mudslide, Mr. Larios, Mr. Barabon, and Jorge Álvarez come with me to dig in the mud where the Arroyos' place used to be. Because it stopped raining an hour or so ago, the mud has begun to dry. By taking soft steps, we can actually walk without sinking down very far. It doesn't take us long to reach the Arroyos'.

For a long time we just stand there, staring at the dark muck. Finally I say to the others, "I think I know about where the store was." I hesitate for a second and point to the ground. "The store was here, but the mud has moved everything back. Look at their roof."

The broken, splintered lumber and metal roofing is scattered on the ground, twenty-five to thirty feet back from the street, as if the storm simply grabbed it and flicked it away. I feel a small rush in my stomach and throat, like I might throw up, but I try to sound calm and sensible. "Maybe the mud pushed everything back. Maybe we should start digging about there," I say, pointing to a spot ten feet or so from where we're standing; this is where I guess the little trucha part of the house might be now. My workmates nod, and we begin digging.

It's hard work. The mud is sloppy and smells bad. Each shovelful seems heavier than the last. The blisters on my hands from digging before, when we were looking for survivors, tear open and start to bleed, but we all keep digging because the last thing we need is to run out of food.

What if we're not even close to where the trucha is?

What if we can't find it?

What if no help comes from the outside, no water, no food, nothing?

What if . . .

I pull up a shovelful of wet mud, and suddenly I see a human hand, its fingers outstretched as though it is reaching toward me.

It looks like a lady's hand.

Mrs. Arroyo.

NINE

It takes a while to get all the mud moved away from Mrs. Arroyo. Not wanting to let the blades of our shovels hit her dead body, each of us is very careful.

When the bodies of little Edgar Barabon and Mrs. Handel were found yesterday, I was with another group at a different spot, so Mrs. Arroyo is the first dead person I have seen other than Mrs. Ramírez, whom I couldn't look at.

Just as we're almost done digging out Mrs. Arroyo's body, Mr. Larios says, "Hold on. Stop."

I ask, "What's wrong?"

He doesn't look at me but keeps staring at the spot

where he's been digging. He sets aside his shovel and kneels down. He carefully moves away some mud with his bare hands. There is another body right next to Mrs. Arroyo's. Now we are digging out Mr. Arroyo too.

The closer we come to getting them out, the worse it smells. None of us says anything, but I fight back gagging. My eyes water and my throat stings. Mr. Barabon and Mr. Larios look sad and sick too. Jorge steps away and retches.

As we get closer and closer to finishing, we see that when the mudslide covered them, the Arroyos were in their bed. They never knew what hit them, except maybe in the final seconds when Mrs. Arroyo reached out. They lie curled up, in sleeping positions, facing away from each other. It looks almost as though they are still just asleep, resting peacefully.

Finally we lift their muddy bodies out and lay them down carefully. I don't want to look at them too closely, but I can't stop myself. You can tell it's them, but they look like wax statues.

So many times I bought treats from Mrs. Arroyo, taking peppermint sticks and strawberry candy from her hand. I remember Mr. Arroyo sweeping in front of their little store and lifting the screen over the open window first thing every morning. Now they are dead!

We lay a black plastic tarp over the Arroyos' bodies and stand over them silently for a few moments, none of us saying anything. As terrible as it is, we must get back to digging for food. I try hard not to look over at the black plastic that covers them. We placed them under the tarp still facing away from each other in death like they were in bed the last night of their lives. I think about my dad and about when he'll come home and cuddle close with my mom in their bed again. What if the Arroyos' bodies were *my* parents? The thought makes me sick.

Finally we start to find some food—two cans of corn and another of green beans. We keep digging. Now it's like finding buried treasure. The Arroyos' little store is full of soggy cardboard box after soggy cardboard box of canned food: hams, Jolly Green Giant vegetables, creamed corn, soups of every type, chili, meat, and canned peaches, pears, and fruit cocktail. But our luckiest finds are the big containers in which the Arroyos stored rice, beans, and flour. Even though these are simple wooden barrels with loose-fitting lids, they were all against a wall that collapsed right over the top of them.

"This is amazing," Mr. Larios says. "All these are still good."

I smile. "Now we have plenty for everyone." As I

say this, I make the mistake of looking again at the black tarp. I immediately feel my face turn red and think, Shut up, stupid!

Mr. Barabon, who has not spoken a single word all morning, notices my embarrassment and says, "It is right to be glad about finding this, José. There is no disrespect. It is good that we found this food, and it is all right to be happy about it. The Arroyos would be the first to say so."

"Thanks," I say.

We are all quiet again.

After more digging, I'm pretty sure that we've found nearly all the food at the Arroyos' trucha. Of course, with all the muck, we can't be sure. But we've found enough to feed La Rupa for many weeks. This is the good news.

The bad news is that even with all this food, in our wet, rainy, muddy world of water, water, and more water, we still don't have much water that we can drink.

TEN

There's no safe water in La Rupa because the sewer pipes burst and contaminated it all. None of our faucets have worked since the night of the storm, and the creek, which runs on the south side of town, was never clean anyway but is now more mud than water. The only flush toilet left in La Rupa is in our house, but since there's no running water and the sewer line's broken, it doesn't flush anymore anyway.

The Rodríguez family has no plumbing, of course. Part of the reason they put their house on the far edge of town was so that their little outhouse would be out of sight in the nearby trees. But that outhouse has filled up now. Everybody has been walking back into the trees for privacy, but raw sewage, from the broken sewer pipes, oozes up out of the mud in the streets. The stench is horrible.

We collect rain in bottles, pots and pans, plastic bags, and any container we can find. But this water is used up as quickly as it's collected. If the rain stops for very long, we'll be in even worse trouble. We found some bottles of juice and soda and one case of bottled water at the Arroyos', but this won't last very long. We have no way of storing a large amount of water anyway, but without it . . .

It's scary to even think about, but how can we not think about it?

Alfredo Mendoza finds a box of his mother's home-canned tomatoes and a large bag of ground corn flour. He looks relieved to see the supply of food we found at the Arroyos'. The Mendozas are probably sharing more than they can really afford to. Alfredo also takes some of our neighbors back to his house to stay. He reminds me that they have a large water tank at his house.

"It is overflowing from all the rain," he tells me. "We have more water than we need."

"So you can give us some, until help arrives," I say, "and we can share our food with you."

Alfredo promises to tell his father about our water shortage.

We are talking out in the street, in front of my house. Alfredo wrinkles his nose and frowns. "What is this smell?"

"Yeah," I say, "it's bad, huh? We think it is mostly the sewage."

"Mostly?" Alfredo asks.

I look down at the mud. "It's probably dead people too."

"Yes," he says quickly, his face red. "I'm sorry."

"It was good of you to bring this food, Alfredo. Please take some of our canned things back in trade."

"Oh no," Alfredo says. "We're all right."

"Please," I say, insisting.

I run back into the house and grab a canned ham and several cans of fruit and milk. When I go back out to the street, I hand them to him.

"This is plenty," Alfredo says. "When we need more, I'll ask for it. Come get some water whenever you are ready."

"Okay."

It's too bad that the Mendoza house is some distance

away. But it's only a ten-minute walk, and we're lucky that it's there at all.

As another night arrives and I go to bed, I start worrying again about Dad and Víctor and Ruby.

Finally I fall asleep and begin to dream. Víctor and I are building rather than tearing down a big brick barbecue on the beach at Omoa. The blue water of the Caribbean laps the shore, and puffy white clouds drift by in the bright-blue sky.

Víctor says, "We'll need this for the storm. The mud will not hurt us, you know." I work eagerly and happily with him, even though a big brick barbecue in the middle of a white beach, with no house, no hut, and nothing anywhere near us doesn't really make much sense.

Ruby is out splashing and swimming in the water. "You're beautiful," I yell. Somehow it doesn't feel funny or awkward to say this to my sister, even if it's something I'd *never* say to her in real life.

Ruby puts her hand up to her ear, signaling that she can't hear me, and then she laughs and dives under the water.

My father walks up to us, carrying three huge lobsters. "La Ceiba crawdaddies," he says, and laughs.

I say, "But there're only three!"

Dad smiles and says, "Three is all we need. Three's plenty."

For some reason I begin to cry. I feel my face burning red and quickly wipe my tears away. But Víctor turns to me and says gently, "It's all right, José. It's okay to be sad, but don't worry, this barbecue will save you all. Don't worry, José."

Now I know that I'm dreaming, because Víctor would never *ever* give me permission to cry. As I think this, Víctor stops his work and looks straight at me. There are tears in his eyes too. "We all cry sometimes, José," he says.

I wake up to an awful rattling sound. At first, still half asleep, I wonder if it's one of the lobsters from my dream, scratching his claws against the red bricks of the barbecue. But now I realize that this rattling sound, horrible, loud, and gasping, is Juan, trying to breathe.

I jump up from my bed and hurry over to his side. His skin is a light grayish color. It looks a little bit like the color of the dead people we saw when we wiped away the mud.

ELEVEN

Mom holds Juan and rocks him quietly. He looks scared and sick. I keep staring at his skin color. We can't find the thermometer to take Juan's temperature, but we know he has a high fever. One moment he sweats, and the next he shakes and quivers from chills. His breathing still makes a bad rattling sound.

I can barely catch a breath myself; my heart pounds so loudly that I wonder if the others can hear it. Juan is so small and weak. I feel so helpless . . . I feel crazy.

"What can I do?" I ask my mom, my voice too loud.

"I don't know," she answers quietly. "We need a doctor."

"I'll go get one," I say, even louder.

"But the nearest doctor is in San Pedro Sula," Mom says.

"Yes," I answer, forcing my voice to be quieter.

"How will you get there?"

"I'll run," I say calmly, and I'm already on my feet, moving toward the door.

Mom says, "No, José, you can't! The bridges probably aren't there anymore, and with all the flooded roads—"

I interrupt, "I'll be careful, but I'm *going*, Mom. I have to!"

Mom says, "José, we need you here, we need—"

Suddenly Ángela, who has been sitting quietly on the couch, listening to us argue, says, "Mamá, José will be okay."

We both look at her. She looks back and forth between Mom and me. "God will not let any harm come to José, Mamá. I know this," she says.

Mom starts to ask, "How can you . . . ?" but she stops and stares into Ángela's eyes.

Ángela says, her voice calm and certain, "I just know, Mamá. God does everything for a reason. We pray to Him to learn what His reasons are and to tell

Him we love Him. God will save José, Mamá . . . I just know it."

Ángela is a kind of odd little girl. She's always very quiet and never says anything unless she has something important to say. She and Juan are close, like María and me, like Víctor and Ruby.

I smile at Ángela and say, "Thanks, Angie." Then I turn to Mom and say, "Ángela is right, Mom. I'll make it. It's what Víctor would do and what Dad would do. I'll be careful, but I *have* to go."

Mom, with tears in her eyes, shakes her head. "But what if . . ." She stops in the middle of her sentence. Now she says, "You promise me that if you can't make it, if it looks too dangerous, you will stop and come back home. Promise me, José. I can't lose you too."

This is the first time Mom has mentioned anything about losing anybody. I understand what she means. "I promise, Mom, but I'll make it. We can't lose Juan either."

Mom says, "Yes, son, that's true."

As I'm getting ready to leave, Mr. Barabon comes up to me. "I'll watch over your mother and sisters and little Juan."

I look him in the eyes and say, "Thanks."

He says, "I'll watch over them until you return or . . ." He hesitates and then says, "I'll take care of them no matter what, no matter how long. I give you my word." He pauses again and says, "Go with God."

I nod.

I grab a plastic bottle full of drinking water.

Ángela looks up from the couch and says, "You'll be safe, José."

I nod again.

Mom gives me one more hug, and I give Juan's arm a little squeeze. His skin is clammy and cold, and it's like he doesn't even notice that I touched him.

I hurry down the street. I'm sinking into the mud a little, but it's nothing like before. The mud has hardened quite a bit, so I run as fast as I can toward the main highway south of town, the road to San Pedro Sula. In some spots, the mud is still softer than in others, and I'm slowed down, sometimes almost tripped. That makes me force myself to go more slowly and be more careful. San Pedro Sula is seventeen miles away. I must pace myself.

I have to make it. I have to get there for Juan.

TWELVE

I've traveled this route to San Pedro Sula on a bus every school day of my life. But it's so different now. What was once thick forest and green pasture is now mud and water, brown and dirty and never ending. Once I'm around a corner and La Rupa is out of sight behind me, I can barely tell which direction to go. The few patches of road not buried in mud are covered in muddy water. Over and over again, I slip off the pavement and feel my ankle turn.

My breaths come faster and faster, not just because I'm tired, but also because I'm afraid. I can't tell exactly where I am. I stop and look around for a land-mark or some sign to guide me. I breathe even faster, and am almost panting as I start to panic.

What would Víctor do right now? I know what he *wouldn't* do: He wouldn't stand here shaking with fear. But I can't help it! If I'm lost, what will happen to Juan? If I can't find my way, what will happen to me?

I'm not Víctor . . . I'm not Dad . . .

But I keep moving, even though nothing looks familiar. The trees that used to line the road are either washed away or bent and broken. They could be any trees, anywhere. All I know is that I keep feel-ing the road under my feet. But is this the right road? Could I have wandered onto one of the side roads that lead in the wrong direction?

I think about Juan again, so sick and pale, about my mom waiting for me to bring back help, about Dad and Víctor and Ruby, maybe dead. No! They aren't dead! They can't be dead. They're alive—they have to be.

The brown water comes up over my ankles. In some places it nearly reaches my knees.

I stop, afraid to go forward and afraid to turn back. I'm not even sure which way *is* forward.

There is a sudden sound off to my right in a tall

clump of bushes, the sound of an animal moving. What kind of animal? Could it be a jaguar? They are the most dangerous predators in all of Honduras. Normally they stay hidden high in the mountains, but with this terrible storm maybe one has come down to hunt, one who hasn't eaten in many days. I look around for a weapon—a stone, a large stick, anything—to help me protect myself, but there is nothing anywhere, only my bare hands!

"Get away!" I yell loudly, my voice stronger than I had imagined possible.

Jaguars are fast, and their spotted coats help them hide until the second before they pounce on their prey.

"Get! Go!" I yell again, my voice weaker and shaking.

There is another loud swooshing sound and a sudden burst of motion from the bushes. Water splashes as the animal makes its charge.

I brace myself, lifting my fists and screaming out.

In another second my scream turns from one of terror to one of total joy. "Berti!" I yell.

Her short fur is mud splattered and matted, her body skinny and soaking wet as she runs as fast as she can toward me. I kneel and she nearly knocks me over, throwing herself into my arms.

"Berti," I cry again.

She doesn't bark but yelps back at me, whining and

whimpering, as excited and happy to see me as I am to see her.

I hold her tightly around her neck, and she wiggles and twists in my arms.

"You okay, girl?" I ask over and over again.

She looks into my eyes. I feel that I can read her mind. She is thinking, I'm back! I'm back! I'm saved!

I hold her and pet her. She quivers in my arms. How long has she been out here, in this area so close to home? What has she eaten? Where has she slept?

I say, "Berti, you're safe now. You're okay. Relax."

We don't leave this spot for a long time, just standing together quietly as I whisper to her, and she calms down.

Although the water is nearly up to Berti's chest at some places, she walks along close to me as we force our way forward. All my fear is gone now. I have to get help for Juan and I will. Berti will help me.

Suddenly I spot, way up ahead, the tall concrete posts at the entry to the Ochoca Bridge. This bridge is three miles outside La Rupa. I can't believe I've traveled this far already. The Ochoca Bridge is on the road that leads to the highway, so we're going the right direction. We're not lost! I feel another burst of energy.

I say to Berti, "There's the bridge! We're almost to the highway. Come on!"

She looks up at me and keeps walking close by.

As we get closer, I see that there is no Ochoca Bridge any longer; the concrete pylons at the entry to the bridge are still here, but the bridge itself is gone. The Ochoca River, which has never been anything more than a slow, lazy, little creek, has become a roaring, muddy torrent.

I stare down at the water rushing by. My energy of a few seconds ago leaves just as fast as it arrived. What am I going to do? It's almost dry up between the pylons—and that's a good thing, because a moment later I've just plopped down onto my butt, too shocked to even stand.

I have to calm down.

My eyes fill with tears, but Berti, panting and wiggling next to me and wagging her tail, stares into my face and licks my cheeks and eyes.

I pet her as I take some slow deep breaths.

After staring at the muddy water for a little while, I realize that although it is going by fast, the river doesn't look very deep.

It starts to rain again, a steady, cold drizzle. I stand up and make my way over to a place on the riverbank that isn't too steep. Berti follows me. Once we are at the river's edge, I look carefully at the spot. This place looks like it's as good as any to try to get across.

"Get across?" I say to Berti. What am I thinking? If I fall, I'll get sucked down and the river will take me away. How can I even think about trying to cross this thing?

"But if we don't go, what happens to Juan?" I ask Berti, who stares back at me. "If I don't go forward, I'll have to go back. And if I stop now, just give up, what do I say to Mom? If I quit and Juan gets sicker . . . what if Juan . . . what if he doesn't get well? How could I ever look at myself in the mirror again?"

Berti stares at me as though she understands every word I'm saying.

Again I realize that this place where I'm standing, just below where the bridge used to be, doesn't look too deep.

Staring at the river, I suddenly see the bodies of a man, a cat, and a dog floating by. The man, thank God, is not Víctor or my dad. He is floating facedown but is wearing a red shirt with bright yellow numbers on the back—a Honduran National Soccer jersey, something Dad and Víctor would never wear. I watch his body floating past—it looks almost like a log, but his arms are stretched out and his hands are a brownish black. Were the dog and cat once friends in this man's life? Family? Did they all die together? In only a few moments they are too far downstream for me to see them anymore.

I look down at Berti, who's also been watching them float away.

I take a deep breath. "You ready, girl?" I ask, taking my first step into the current. Berti steps forward too but stops suddenly. I say, "Come on, Berti. We can do this," but she is staring intently across the river.

Now I hear what she has already heard, a sudden loud sound. Seconds later, roaring and splashing into the river from the opposite bank, only a short distance downstream, is a camouflage-colored military truck marked *United Nations Relief*. Another truck just like it follows, and behind it is a third truck with big red crosses on its side and hood. All three trucks splash into the river and begin to power their way across.

For a few seconds I just stand here. The splash of the first vehicle sprays out. Suddenly I grasp what the red cross means: This is a medical truck! They can help Juan!

I run along the bank, waving my arms. The soldiers in the first truck don't see me. I wave my arms harder and almost fall down as I begin to holler, "*¡Mi hermano está enfermo!*" I yell as loud as I can in

Spanish, and the same thing in English, even louder: "My brother is sick!"

I stumble over the round river rocks, and I can barely hear my own voice over the trucks' roaring engines. Berti runs ahead of me, silent and agile, flying over the stones. The two men in the first vehicle still don't see me, but I look at the driver of the second truck and at a man and woman in the third one. They stare straight at Berti and me.

As they come out of the river, the second and third trucks stop abruptly and honk their horns to the lead truck. It stops too. Blue exhaust pours out from their tailpipes, and steam rises from around the engines.

I run up to the second vehicle and say in English, "My brother . . ." I'm breathing too hard to speak. "My brother sick . . ." I can't seem to catch my breath. "My brother is very sick . . . very . . . he's very sick . . . can you come to help me?"

The soldier sitting in the passenger seat says in English, "You speak English?" He sounds surprised. He doesn't sound American. His accent is strange to me.

"Yes," I answer. "I'm a student at the International School. I speak English very well." I gasp for breath.

"Calm down. You're doing fine," the driver says. "You've got a brother who's sick?"

"Yes!" I say, almost yelling. "My little brother Juan is very sick! Are you a doctor?"

"I'm not. Captain Albertson is the doc." He nods toward the Red Cross truck behind him. "He's in the next rig back. I'm not sure we can help you right now, though, son."

Not help? How can this be? My mouth goes dry and I can't think of a single word in English. If this captain is a doctor, surely he will help. He *has* to help!

"But my brother is *very* sick," I blurt out. "There are many dead in my *pueblo*. . . . My brother will be dead if I don't bring help."

"Talk to the captain, lad," says the soldier driving the truck.

I hurry back to the truck with the red crosses on it. A woman soldier is driving and a man soldier with gold bars on his shoulders sits next to her. He has a kind face, which is good because he is a *huge* man— he must be twice my height and three times my weight. He has red hair and blue eyes and freckles.

I force myself to speak. "Are you the captain doctor?"

"Yes," he answers kindly, smiling at me. "You speak English, eh?" He doesn't sound American either—his English sounds strange, like that of the soldiers in the other truck.

I ask, "Where are you here from?"

He smiles and says, "We're with U.N. International Relief. Our squadron is multinational, but I'm from Edinburgh, Scotland."

I say, "My brother is very sick. He needs help right away!"

"I'm sorry," the doctor says, "but we're under strict orders—"

"But my brother is just a baby . . ." I feel tears building up in the back of my throat and at the corners of my eyes. I fight them back. What would Víctor do? What would Dad say? Berti, maybe sensing my mood, rubs against my leg, wagging her tail.

"I'm sorry," the doctor says again, and I can tell that he *is* truly sorry, "but we're under strict orders to go to . . ." He turns to the lady soldier who is behind the steering wheel. "Where is it, Lieutenant?"

She says, "Las . . . Las Ruppa?" pronouncing it wrong.

"La Rupa?" I ask.

"Yes," the doctor says. "La Rupa. Do you know where it is?"

"Yes," I say quickly. "Yes, I know *exactly* where La Rupa is."

THIRTEEN

Berti sits in the backseat of the truck, and I sit up front, telling them everything—about the rains, the power failure, the mudslide, the water, the food, the Arroyos and all the other dead, and my brother Juan. I try to speak slowly and clearly, and I struggle to remember all the right words in English.

"Jesus," the doctor says, "you really been through it, haven't ya?"

I nod.

He tells me about San Pedro Sula and the other parts of Honduras that he has seen: towns under

90

water, thousands of people waiting on the roads to be rescued, and the horrible damage across the whole country. He tells me about the shelters overflowing with people, so many of them homeless, and about some children stuck on a rooftop for three days and nights after their parents were lost in the flood.

He says, "People in La Ceiba are fishing from their front porches, catching fish and crawdads from what used to be the streets."

"La Ceiba!" I gasp.

"Yes. You have people there?"

I take a deep breath and explain, "My dad and my older brother, Víctor, and my sister haven't come back from there yet."

And now I start rambling, saying crazy-sounding stuff, one stupid thing after another: I talk about Víctor tearing down the barbecue, about Ruby and her modeling portfolio, about my dad and his truck, and about Berti being lost. I know I sound crazy, but I can't seem to keep from babbling.

I force myself to slow down, saying, "Of course, maybe they are all right. Maybe they are staying with people somewhere. Maybe they are—" Suddenly I begin to sob. Ashamed, I turn my head away and stare out the window so that they won't see me cry.

From the corner of my eye I see Berti, standing and staring straight at me, worried and protective.

The doctor asks, "What kind of truck does your father drive?"

"A medium-sized one," I say.

I keep staring out the window, but I hear the doctor's soft smile in his voice. "No, José. I mean, what make, what model, what color is it?"

"It is a white Volvo truck—a large van. It is four years old, 1994, perhaps a '93." It says *Cruz Reparto* on each side in bright-blue letters."

"Very good, José," the doctor says. He picks up the microphone attached to the radio on the dashboard. "This is MEDRUN eight-niner. Come in."

The radio crackles. "Acknowledge, MEDRUN eight-niner—identify."

"Captain Albertson, Unit eight-niner."

"Acknowledge. State your purpose, sir."

Captain-Doctor Albertson speaks clearly and directly with an official sound to his words. "We're approximately three kilometers outside the village of La Rupa. Have encountered and enlisted support of English-speaking Honduran national to assist in translation. Over."

"Copy that, sir. Over."

"Need an all-alert priority search and seek, three

Honduran nationals. Identities: Señor . . ." He pauses a second, letting his thumb slip off the button on the microphone, and turns to me. "What is your father's full name?"

"Alberto Cruz," I say.

The doctor clicks the button of the microphone again. "Señor Alberto Cruz and two teenaged children . . ."

As the doctor talks into his radio, he asks me for descriptions of what Dad and Víctor and Ruby were wearing, their height and weight, and all kinds of questions. I answer as best I can remember. The doctor passes all this information along.

The radio crackles again. "Copy all and roger that, sir. Good luck in La Rupa. It sounds pretty ugly out there."

The doctor glances at me, looking a little embarrassed. "Affirmative. We'll check back at eleven hundred hours and provide update on mission status. Signing off."

"Signing off, sir."

The radio goes silent. I say, "Thank you, doctor. Thank you so much."

"It's the least we can do for our new translator," he says, his voice kind and gentle. "You will help us, right?"

"Absolutamente," I answer. "Sorry. I mean, absolutely, yes, of course!"

We arrive at the southern entrance to La Rupa. The three trucks slowly inch forward. Seeing the damage, I am stunned all over again. I'll never get used to this new La Rupa.

We move past the Rodríguezes' little shack. The people standing and sitting there watch us in silence. No one looks surprised to see me in the truck with these soldiers. No one looks happy or scared or anything, really—just numb. Some of the people begin to walk cautiously toward us.

Silently I say a prayer for Dad and Víctor and Ruby. "Please, God, let my family be okay . . . please let them come home to us . . ."

As I look at what's left of La Rupa, I have a sick feeling. I say another prayer, this one soft but out loud. "Please, God, let Juan be okay . . . please, God . . . please, God, don't let us be too late."

Before the truck even comes to a full stop, Berti bounds out. But instead of running to the house, she stands still, looking at me and waiting for me to come to her.

FOURTEEN

Lieutenant Sally parks the truck where the mud makes it impossible to drive any farther. How long until the doctor can see Juan? I try to mentally will us to hurry up the muddy street to our house.

As we get out of the truck, Dr. Albertson asks, "Where is your brother?"

"That is our home," I answer, pointing up the street. "Juan is there with my mother and many more people."

"Let's go!" Dr. Albertson says.

As we walk, Dr. Albertson calls to his nurse,

95

Lieutenant Sally. They talk quietly together as we hurry up the muddy road. They wear boots with thick treads, so they are able to pass through the mud more quickly than I can. I struggle to keep up. Berti stays by my side. The doctor and nurse pause at the door to my house, waiting for me and Berti to catch up.

I step past them and walk into the living room. Everybody looks up at me and at the Anglo doctor and the nurse.

I say in Spanish, "This is Captain Dr. Albertson and Lieutenant Nurse Sally. They've come to help us. They don't speak Spanish, but I'll help."

I look around for my mother and Juan, but they're not here.

"Where's Juan?" I try to ask, but the words stick in my throat.

Mom, carrying Juan on her hip, steps into the room from her bedroom. Juan looks pale and tired, but he's awake and quiet; he stares straight at us. In his right hand he carries C-3PO. I smile at Juan, but his eyes look glassy. He doesn't smile back, but he says in a weak voice, "Berti, you came home!"

Berti wags her tail.

"Pneumonia," Dr. Albertson says to me.

I translate for Mom, who looks very worried.

Dr. Albertson sees Mom's reaction and quickly adds, "He's going to be just fine. I've given him enough antibiotics to cure a whole village. In situations like this, where there is so much dampness and dirt, bronchitis and pneumonia are quite common. But your little brother is strong, and we got to him early. He needs bed rest and fluids, but he'll be okay."

My eyes sting again. Thanks, God, I say to myself.

Nurse Sally says to me, "You did well, José. I'm so glad you found us and helped us get here. Good work." Her kind words make me feel good, but embarrassed too.

I mutter, "I'm just glad you were coming here." Dr. Albertson smiles at us. Watching him work with Juan, I notice again how large the doctor's hands are as he gently takes Juan's tiny arm and lifts it up.

Dr. Albertson says to me, "It's lucky we met you. The translator for our team, Sergeant Pérez, is on leave. His wife is having a baby. He'll be catching up with us next week, but in the meantime we weren't sure how we were going to manage. You've helped us as much as we've helped you."

This man saved Juan. He can do no wrong in my eyes.

Now the doctor asks me to translate his words to my mother.

"Mrs. Cruz, you have good boys here," he says, smiling. I'm a little embarrassed to translate this. The doctor sees my hesitation. "Tell her exactly what I said, José."

I follow his orders, and my mother smiles and nods. He says, "Mrs. Cruz, you've done a wonderful job helping your neighbors. Now I need to ask you to do even more."

Dr. Albertson pauses to allow for my translation to catch up. Mom nods as I talk. When I've finished speaking, he adds, "Your home looks like the only secure structure in La Rupa. We need to set up an emergency clinic here just for today. Is that all right with you?"

As I finish my translation, Mom nods and says *"Sí, claro."*

I translate her words: "Yes, of course."

"Thank you, ma'am," Dr. Albertson says. "I know that you have family out and unaccounted for. We've put out a search for them, and I'll keep you posted of any developments."

Mom listens to my translation and just nods and says, *"Gracias."* There is no change in her expression.

Watching them talk, I'm surprised all over again by how strong and brave my mother is. Mom is just over five feet in height, yet she looks up directly at this tall soldier as he speaks. She doesn't speak English, but she listens carefully to him and watches his expressions, and then listens just as carefully to my translations of his words. She doesn't show how worried she really must be.

The doctor and Nurse Sally begin to move people from one side of the room to another, and Nurse Sally calls out to the other soldiers to hurry and bring up the medical supplies.

"You're first," she says to me.

"Why? I'm fine. I'm not hurt."

"Oh, really?" she asks. "These wounds are normal for you?" I look at the spots she points to on my arms and ankles—cuts, scratches, and ugly red splotches on my skin. I honestly hadn't even noticed them until this moment.

Nurse Sally raises her voice, speaking loudly enough so that Dr. Albertson will hear her. "The doctor will tell you these splotches are impetigo. And it's important to clean up the cuts and abrasions, especially with so much infection possible." Her voice goes even higher. "Doctors love to think that they're the only ones who know such things."

Dr. Albertson chuckles at her words. He stands at the new pharmacy in the corner of our living room and says over his shoulder, "And nurses, especially when they are outranked, love to think that they know as much as their superiors."

Nurse Sally laughs too.

Sitting in a chair, Nurse Sally begins to dab my cuts and scratches with medicine. It stings. "Ouch!"

Berti suddenly gets up and hurries over, walking in between us, kind of nudging Nurse Sally away from me.

Nurse Sally looks at Berti and says, "It's okay, doggy. I'm not going to hurt your master."

I say to Berti, "It's okay, girl."

Berti stares up at me but doesn't move.

Ángela and María are standing near the hallway to the back of the house. I call to María.

"What, José?"

"Why don't you and Ángela take Berti to the backyard and rinse some of the mud off her?"

Ángela asks, "Can we use the water for that?"

Dr. Albertson says, "Don't use too much, but we've brought a lot of bottled water along, so a little bit would be fine."

María calls, "Come on, Berti."

Berti doesn't move. She just stares up at me again.

"Go ahead, Berti," I say. "Go with María and Ángela. You need to get cleaned up too. Go."

María taps her hand on her leg and says, "Come, Berti."

Berti slowly walks over to my sisters, who gently take her by the collar and lead her out the back door.

Nurse Sally finishes cleaning and disinfecting the many scratches and small cuts all over my hands, arms, and ankles. She is gentle, and after that first tiny stinging, the medicine hardly hurts.

I translate for the doctor and nurse as they help everyone else. Mr. Barabon gets bandages for his cut and bruised hands; he says nothing about his two dead children. Mr. Handel, his back bent and his ankle horribly swollen, says nothing about these injuries, nor does he mention losing his wife.

Soon everyone in the village is lined up, sitting or standing quietly, waiting to see the doctor. The children get shots. None of them cry, not even the littlest ones like Miguel Cortez, who lost his mom in the mudslide.

Dr. Albertson tells each patient, "It might be a while before we can get back here. You have to avoid infections and illness the best you can. You must try to stay healthy."

"Yes," Nurse Sally adds, "and boil, boil, boil your water, unless it comes straight from a bottle."

The day drags on. There are several broken fingers and one broken hand, but the problems are mostly sprains and the beginnings of sickness, coughs, and runny noses. No one complains, no one loses their dignity. I'd been so worried about Juan getting sick, and about Dad and Víctor and Ruby, that I hadn't really noticed how many other people were injured.

When the doctor is finally finished with the last patient, one of the soldiers comes in to talk with him. I go to the front door and look out at the town. The soldiers have set up large tents. The sides are rolled up, so I can see inside. There are cots, cooking stoves, cans of cooking fuel, big bottles of water, and packets of food. These shelters are for all the people who have been staying with us, at the Rodríguez place, and with Alfredo's family. There are six large tents with enough room for everyone who needs to stay in one. These soldiers have shown us that we are not alone, that La Rupa has not been forgotten.

Back inside my house, I overhear what the soldier is saying to Dr. Albertson.

"There is nothing more we can do today, sir. We need to head back to San Pedro Sula for the night."

Dr. Albertson nods to the soldier and then turns to me and says, "We'll be back as soon as we can, José."

"Thank you," I say.

"Later in the week," he adds. "Next week at the latest."

They've done so much for us, but all I can say is "Thank you," again.

"Sure . . ." Dr. Albertson begins, and then says, "Of course, if I receive any word about your father and the others . . ." He pauses for a second, looking over at Mom, then back to me. "If I hear anything, I'll get word to you immediately."

I translate his words to Mom. She gives a little smile, but there are tears in her eyes.

FIFTEEN

Berti and I are standing together in the backyard and I speak to her softly so that only she can hear me. "I wonder what we're going to do now. How will we ever clean up all this mud? And what about the dead people? We haven't even buried them yet."

I know, of course, that Berti doesn't understand my words, but she seems to sense what I'm feeling. It's amazing how good it feels to have her back.

Just before they leave, the U.N. soldiers tell us that the Honduran military will come later today to help us.

They explain that the dead will have to be dug out and then burned in order to avoid the spread of disease.

The Honduran soldiers arrive just before nightfall. They come in four beat-up old Honduran military trucks and two small tractors and a backhoe. The tractors' engines sputter to life. The backhoe moves slowly toward where the Cortez house used to be. I smell the blue diesel smoke. Mom, María, Ángela, Juan, and I are alone in our house again. Our neighbors have moved into their new tent homes.

We sit listening to the machines tear up the ground, searching for lost souls. They don't stop until ten o'clock at night.

Finally everyone buried in the mud has been accounted for and recovered. Each of the dead has been identified by a family member or, if a whole family was killed, by one or more of the neighbors. The soldiers have wrapped the bodies in plain brown cloths, tied with ropes, and carefully laid them, side by side, on the road.

All of us gather around, and each person who wishes to speaks for lost loved ones.

Mr. Altunez says to the dead body of his wife, "Good-bye, dear. We love you." He is too choked up to say more. Both Carlos and Pablo are sobbing.

Mr. Handel says, "Rest in peace, my son and my daughter. Rest in peace, Rosa . . . my love." Now he is weeping too hard to say more.

No one speaks for very long. The soldiers all stand in a line, their green caps held over their hearts and their heads bowed. One of them is crying. They all wait respectfully, but they have much to do.

For the Marpaleses, the Hernándezes, and the Arroyos, since every member of the family was killed, an army chaplain speaks. "Dear friends, dear neighbors, we will remember you always and pray for you. Rest in peace now. Let us pray. Our father who art in heaven . . ."

We all pray together. Soon everyone goes back to their tents. Mom, María, Ángela, and Juan go back to our house, where Berti lies on the porch waiting for us. But I wait awhile longer, standing by where the bodies are, saying my final good-byes. I watch as the soldiers gently load the dead into a large truck and then take them to a field southwest of town, a quarter mile away.

One Honduran soldier, the last one still in town, asks me gently, "Did you lose anyone here?"

He is a young guy, maybe just older than Víctor, but he looks grown-up in his dark-green Honduran army uniform. He has darker skin than I do, and his features look Indian. He's handsome and his voice is kind.

I answer, "No, I have no dead family here, just friends and neighbors." I add, "My father and older brother and sister . . ." I pause and take a quick breath. ". . . they are missing."

He looks away from me. "I'm sorry."

"Yes," I answer. Then I quickly add, "We still hope to hear from them."

"I understand." The young soldier nods but still doesn't look me in the eye.

"What you do must be very difficult," I say.

He hesitates and then says, "We do what has to be done when we burn the bodies from the fields and rivers and—" Suddenly he stops and looks at me. "I'm sorry," he says. "I didn't mean—"

I interrupt, "No, it's okay. I understand. You're doing a hard job and you're helping us. Don't feel bad."

The soldier nods. "I have to go," he says.

"Sure," I say. He walks toward his truck, climbs up, and glances back at me. I yell over the rumbling of his truck's engine, "Good luck and thank you."

"You too," he says, and waves good-bye.

I watch him drive away, but I can't stop thinking

about what he just said to me: "when we burn the bodies from the fields and rivers." I remember what the radio said about the thousands of people missing.

What about Dad and Víctor and Ruby? How many people will never be identified, if their bodies are pulled from the rivers and fields and burned without anyone knowing who they are? I try to force myself away from these thoughts—but I keep thinking *missing, missing, missing*. Where's my father? My brother? My sister?

Are they lost forever?

SIXTEEN

In the darkness, Mom, Ángela, María, and I stand on the steps at our front door. Juan is asleep already, but the rest of us watch the yellow-orange flames of the soldiers' fire.

After a while, I notice that María has moved closer to me. I can't remember the last time I spoke to María since all this started.

María says softly, "They aren't burning life. They're burning death."

I look at her and nod. Then I put my arm around her shoulders. "I know," I say as she slips her arm around my back. I can't think of another time in our lives when María and I have held each other like this. It feels good. As the next oldest to me in age, María is to me like Ruby was to Víctor . . . I mean *is* to Víctor!

Ángela and Mom stand quietly.

Our friends and neighbors stand outside their tents watching the fire as well. These moments—the hurried service by the side of the road and now this fire on the edge of town—are as close to a funeral as they will have for their loved ones. I feel so sad for everyone, for the dead *and* those of us left behind.

Looking at the fire, Mom says, "Pray for them, for their souls."

Ángela asks, "What should I say? What words?"

"Whatever words your heart tells you. Or the Rosary. Pray what feels right to you."

María begins to whisper softly, "Our father who art in heaven, hallowed be thy name . . ."

I pray too, but just to myself. *God, if you're really there, if you're listening . . . I don't know why you sent us this. I don't understand.* I stop. Maybe God will be angry at me for what I'm feeling and saying. I'm so tired and confused that I can't even pray right.

Please, Jesus, help us. I pray for the Arroyos; I pray for Vera Ramírez, for Allegra Barabon, and for all the dead people. I pray for Ruby and for Víctor and for

Dad. *God, please let Dad and Víctor and Ruby be all right. I'm begging you, please just let my family be all right!*

Berti, who has been lying quietly in a corner of the living room, walks over and lies down at my feet.

I watch the flames against the dark sky, bodies from La Rupa burning.

It is the most horrible thing I've ever seen.

An hour later, with Berti once again sleeping on her blanket at the end of my bed, I fall asleep.

My dreams are confused. Some are nice, like seeing Ruby eating an apple and laughing at something Dad has said. Mom laughs too. This actually happened in real life—Ruby and the apple and Dad and Mom. Everything is just like it was.

In my next dream, Víctor stands next to me where the stack of bricks used to be in our yard. He points to the huge boulder that rolled so close to the house. "What is this?" he asks angrily.

Víctor points at the bricks scattered around in the mud. "Damn it, we'll have to fix this," he says. Then, smiling, he adds, "Hail Mary, full of grace . . . damn it!" Then he laughs. Although I somehow know I'm dreaming, I almost cry because it feels so good to hear my brother laugh again.

* * *

When I wake up in the morning, only one thought is in my mind: I have to find Dad and Víctor and Ruby. I have to find them!

Mom says, "No! Absolutely not! You're not leaving again! Can't you see how much I need you here?"

Of course, I know that her needing my help is not the real reason she doesn't want me to go; she's worried for me.

I say, very softly and calmly, "I'll be careful, Mom. I'll come back every night, but I have to look for them. Maybe they're already hurt. Maybe they need help. I have to try."

Mom says, "The soldiers are looking. They have helicopters, trucks, and hundreds of people. What can you do that they aren't doing?"

I say, "Mom, the soldiers have too much to do and too many people to look for. They don't *know* us. They won't search the way that I will."

I don't tell Mom what I'm most afraid of, that the soldiers might find Dad and Víctor and Ruby dead in some river or some field and not know who they are and burn them, and that we'll never know what happened. Thinking this makes me crazy.

Mom's quiet for a moment. Then she says softly, "You may be right, José. I know you would try hard to find them, but I need you *here*."

I look at her face. Something's changed between us. There's a new kind of trust. I know that she needs me, and she will especially if Dad and Víctor and Ruby are . . . if they don't come back.

I say, "You're right, Mom. I'll wait a little while, another day or two until things are better." But we both know that nothing will be better in a day or two. We see this in each other's eyes. Still, I can give her this much. I'll wait a few days, but then I'll have to go.

SEVENTEEN

On the morning of this fifth day after the mudslide, a group of us are shoveling in the street, trying to get it cleaned up enough so that cars will be able to drive through town again. Mr. Barabon, Mr. Cortez, and Mr. Ramírez are with me, along with Jorge Álvarez and Pablo and Carlos Altunez. We work slowly, shoveling mud and drying dirt to the sides of the road. I feel almost good. The blisters on my hands are turning to calluses and I feel strong. It's sunny, and the warmth on my shoulders feels nice; it reminds me of tearing down the barbecue that day with Víctor, the

114

day when everyone watched us. That seems like a million years ago. I wish I had kept on helping my brother that day. I'd give anything if Víctor were here now, the two of us working together.

The morning passes slowly. Although there isn't much laughter among us, we talk quietly to one another.

Mr. Barabon says to me, "You were right about the food, about the Arroyos' store. It's good we had you to show us where to look."

I smile at him and answer, "Going to the Arroyos' store was my mom's idea. Besides, I was just lucky."

Mr. Cortez says, "No, José, luck had nothing to do with it. You are your father's son. You figured out the perfect spot for us to dig. You're smart and hard-working. You're becoming a good man."

I feel my face redden. It feels weird to hear these grown-ups talking to me like this, but I've noticed the other grown-ups listening to me more too, treating me almost like I'm a leader.

Mr. Barabon says, "You're the man of your house now, José. You're doing a good job. The way you went and found the doctor, your English—you are helping all of us."

"Thanks," I say, but I feel funny hearing this. I'm proud that he is complimenting me, but I am *not* the man of our house. Dad is, and Víctor will be some-day. I don't want to think about this. . . .

After digging for a while longer, I hear a truck coming into town. We've made good progress and have cleared almost fifty yards. The truck stops near us and Dr. Albertson climbs out. I'm happy to see him again.

He walks directly toward me. *"Hola,"* he says warmly. But his face looks sad. He looks me right in the eyes and says, "We've found the truck, José."

At first I don't know what he's talking about. I ask, "The truck? You've found the . . ." Now it hits me: He means my father's truck. I want to ask where, but I can't seem to find the word in English. *"¿Dónde?"* is all I can say, but he doesn't speak Spanish. I feel light-headed. Looking at his face, I almost want to say, "Please don't say any more."

He says, "When the bridge was washed out over the Conrejal River on this side of La Ceiba, the truck was swept away. I'm so sorry."

"Swept away?" I ask.

The doctor pauses and glances away and then back at me. "The truck was taken by the river when the water knocked down the bridge."

"Yes," I say. "Swept away, but . . . what about Dad

and Víctor and Ruby? Did you find them?"

He looks down and takes a slow breath. He doesn't want to speak, but he makes himself continue. "They weren't in the truck when they found it, but all the windows were broken out and the rig was submerged."

I feel a crazy surge of hope. "Maybe they're okay then! I mean, if the windows were broken out and—"

"They might be," Dr. Albertson interrupts, "but I'm not going to lie to you. It's far more likely that they drowned and that the current carried them away."

"Are you sure it's my dad's truck?"

"I'm afraid so, José." He hesitates and says, "We retrieved some things from the vehicle."

"What things?" I ask.

"Personal items." The doctor stops and then asks, "I know this is hard, but are you up to taking a look?"

"Yes," I say, but my voice comes out weak and squeaks.

We walk to the truck, and the doctor reaches in through the open window. He grabs a green plastic army bag with a ziplock top and hands it to me. I open it slowly and look inside.

Immediately, I recognize Ruby's shoe. Even though it is covered in mud, I see the Nike swoosh. The shoes were Ruby's pride and joy. My legs feel weak and I'm dizzy. I empty the rest of the bag onto the hood of the truck. There are papers, soaked through and caked with mud but still partially readable—a registration certificate, insurance documents, a business license in my dad's name. Víctor's leather wallet is here too. I pick it up. Although it's wet, it looks okay. I keep clutching it. "It's so perfect," I mumble. "Víctor's wallet is in perfect shape."

Dr. Albertson says, "I noticed that too. These other papers"—he points to the soggy mess—"they were attached to the visor and . . ."

I don't hear the rest because I suddenly feel a wave of sickness wash over me. I put my hand on the hood of the truck to try to keep myself from falling down. Víctor's wallet, Ruby's shoe—these details are so unimportant, so useless, yet they mean so much.

My hand begins to slide along the smooth green metal. The doctor sees me starting to fall. He reaches over and grabs my arm, holds me up, and steadies me.

"You okay?" he asks.

I nod, taking deep breaths.

He says, "I could be wrong, José. I hope to God I am. Maybe the windows being broken means they *did* get out; maybe they didn't drow—" He doesn't finish the word or his sentence. Instead he says softly, "Maybe they're okay."

My mother takes the news quietly. Dr. Albertson doesn't tell her as many details as he told me. I translate as he explains that the truck has been found but that Dad and Víctor and Ruby are still missing.

Mom says, "We will just keep praying." That's all she says. I'm proud of her for being so strong, yet I'm also embarrassed to translate this to the doctor. Maybe he'll think we're just silly and superstitious. But when I tell him what my mother has said, he nods and takes her hand in his. He says, "I'll pray too, Mrs. Cruz."

After Dr. Albertson leaves, Mom quietly goes back to her chores. I slump down at the kitchen table. I sit there for a long time, not moving, not thinking, not feeling.

After a while I go out and stand next to the big boulder. I think about all the prayers I've said, all the Our Fathers, all the Hail Marys. What a waste of time! I raise my right fist and punch the rock. Pain shoots through my hand and up my arm, but I pull back and hit it again and again. Blood trickles from the open skin on my knuckles. I drag the wounds across the stone, leaving streaks of smeared blood.

I feel like murdering the whole world.

EIGHTEEN

I join the others still shoveling mud from the street, but it's like a fog surrounds me. The others understood about Dad's truck. No one looks me in the eye. As I shovel, I'm quiet. Mr. Barabon and Jorge Álvarez, who are shoveling closest to me, must see something in my face that makes them quiet too.

I think back to a time last year when I went with Dad to La Ceiba. It was just the two of us. All along the road that day, we saw flock after flock of wild parrots, their feathers green, red, and yellow.

"They fly so beautifully," I said.

"Yes, they really do," my dad said. Then he smiled and added, "They are Honduras."

"What do you mean?" I asked.

Dad, still watching the road, said, "I was in the United States once when I was a young man. I traveled around a little bit and saw many wonderful sights, some of the great cities like New York and Los Angeles, much of the countryside, many mountains and rivers, and all of that space."

"I didn't know that, Dad."

Dad smiled. "I know. It was before I even met your mother. I was a young man then, and it was my great adventure."

"Wow," I said.

Dad glanced over at me. "But in all the places I visited, José, never once, nowhere in North America, did I see wild parrots like we have here. They may live there someplace, but I never saw them, and I missed them so much that I couldn't wait to get back home." He smiled at me and laughed.

I tried to figure out why Dad was telling me this.

Then he added, "We're Hondurans, son. This is a good thing . . . a *great* thing. It doesn't matter how big your country is. It doesn't even really matter whether you have wild parrots. What matters is what kind of man you become. But I'll be truthful with you: I'd never want to live someplace where there are no parrots flying free."

In that moment I knew exactly what my Dad was saying. After that day wild parrots never looked the same to me again. They were always more beautiful.

I go back to shoveling and force myself to think about other things. But I can't stop thinking about Dad and Víctor and Ruby, and soon another memory comes, a memory of something that happened just a couple of weeks ago. I had walked into the kitchen, and Víctor and Ruby were sitting at the table, eating chips and talking.

"I never said that I 'loved' her," Víctor said, laughing as he threw a chip at Ruby.

Grabbing the chip and munching it, Ruby said to him, "You didn't have to say it, big boy. Look at your face!"

Víctor blushed and laughed. "How am I supposed to look at my face?"

I jumped in. "You could look in the mirror," I said. They both looked at me and burst out laughing.

"What?" I asked. "What'd I say?"

Víctor said, "That's right, José . . . a mirror. I'm sure I'd have never thought of that."

I felt like an idiot, but Ruby looked at me and

could see that my feelings were hurt. She punched Víctor in the arm and said, "You stop it." Then she turned to me. "You're right, José, he *could* look in a mirror. He's just jealous because you're so smart." They both laughed again, and despite myself, I laughed too.

Nobody in the world could make Víctor and me laugh the way that Ruby could.

I mean the way she *can*. I won't believe she's dead, that Dad and Víctor and Ruby are dead.

I glance at the knuckles on my right hand, at the scabs and dried blood from when I hit the rock. I'm *glad* that my hand stings, *glad* that it hurts. It takes my mind off the pain I feel inside.

I'm sweaty from all the shoveling. The sun warms my shoulders and beats down on my head. I stop for a moment to rest and look up at the sunny blue sky. There is a perfect rainbow. The colors are clear and bright, red, green, and yellow like a parrot's wings. For a crazy second I have the feeling that this rainbow is a message from Dad. He's telling me that he and Víctor and Ruby are somewhere up there in the sky, happy and safe and flying with the wild parrots.

I feel this terrible, sad, happy ache. But now the happiness part leaves and I just feel sad. I don't want them with the parrots. I don't want them dead. I want them back home.

It's dinnertime, but after the news about Dad's truck, I'm not hungry at all. I know I should make myself eat, but I keep seeing Dad and Víctor and Ruby being pulled from the river and then burned in a great pile of unknown bodies. I move the rice and beans around my plate with my fork and stare at the mess. I'd rather throw this plate against the wall than take another bite. Mom stares at me, but I don't look back. I finally manage to eat a little, but I don't taste it. I can barely get it down without gagging.

How could this happen? A few days ago all I could think about was school and sports. My favorite ice cream flavor was chocolate. I used to imagine that someday I'd travel around the world and see great places, like my Dad did when he was young. But that was then, a thousand years ago, a million lifetimes ago. Nothing's possible now.

How could God do this to Dad and to my brother and sister? I don't understand. I don't understand any of it.

NINETEEN

My sleep last night was angry. I can't remember my dreams, but I wake up this morning with a feeling of dread.

I dress quickly and go into the living room. At least the sun is out again, shining brightly through our big front window like it did yesterday.

Mom is already up and in the kitchen getting breakfast ready. "Good morning, José."

I answer, "Hi."

She calls toward the bedrooms to the other kids, "Let's go! It's delivery time!"

María comes out and stands next to me, rubbing the sleep out of her eyes.

Ángela and Juan straggle out a few moments later.

Mom is talking about the rice and beans and flour we got from the Arroyos' trucha. It's still being stored at our house, and Mom has us deliver supplies each morning before our own breakfasts to all the tents and the Rodríguez place.

Ángela asks, "How long do we have to do this, Mom?"

Mom answers, "Until our neighbors have something more than canvas walls to protect them."

Mom has already filled the plastic bags for us.

María and I are the *real* delivery people. Ángela and Juan are too little to help much. In fact, Juan's "help" always makes the job twice as hard as it would be if I just did it myself. But I let him help anyway, just like Víctor always used to let me help him when I was little.

María and Ángela deliver the food to the closer tents. I go to the three tents farthest away from our home and to the Rodríguez place. I have twelve bags in all. Juan "carries" the bags in my left hand with me.

I'm walking down the middle of the street, down the wide path we've shoveled clear, when I first hear and then see a military truck coming slowly into town. Lots of trucks have been here over the last two days, so I am not surprised by this one. It could be bringing water, or maybe they're coming back to start work on the sewer lines or the phones or the electricity.

Suddenly a small flock of only three parrots zooms over my head and up toward what's left of the hillside. They are the first birds I've seen since the mudslide. They land on a broken tree, where the rainbow was when we were shoveling yesterday. I smile, but the good feeling doesn't last. What do I care about wild parrots anymore? What difference do they make? The plastic bags I'm carrying feel heavy. I'll be glad when I'm done with this stupid chore.

I kick a stone that's lying in the street, but part of it's stuck in the ground, so it doesn't move. I look back at the truck, which is still slowly moving toward me. Maybe it's Dr. Albertson and Nurse Sally, not that I care anymore. Besides, from this distance I can tell that it is a Honduran army rig. It's older than the U.N. trucks and moves like a snail.

I have reached the Barabon tent. My hands ache from the weight of the bags. I holler, "Hello!"

Mrs. Barabon calls back to me, "Good morning. Come in." She steps up to the flap and smiles at me.

"Hi, Juan," she says. Juan stands close to me, holding my leg.

Juan says, "Hi," and smiles at her.

She pats Juan on the head. A few days ago, she lost her daughter, Allegra, and her son, Edgar. There is a horrible sadness in her eyes.

I look away, feeling bad and sorry for her.

Mrs. Barabon glances over my shoulder and suddenly her eyes open wide. "My God!" she says. "Look behind you, José!"

I glance back at the truck again. It's close now, close enough so that I can see the people inside. The driver is a soldier, but there are two passengers with him. I stare . . . blinking hard and squinting. . . . I keep staring, afraid to look away for even a second. I drop all the bags to the ground. The one with the rice breaks open.

Looking at the spilled rice, Juan says, "Uh-oh . . . ," letting go of my leg.

I run as fast as I can toward the truck, tripping and almost falling down. My heart pounds inside my chest. Words catch in my throat. I laugh and yell— not words, just loud hollering. Seated next to the soldier is my dad, and beside him, now leaning out the window and smiling at me, is Víctor!

TWENTY

Tears stream down my face as I reach the passenger door.

Víctor, trying to sound stern, says, "What're you crying about?" Then he smiles again. I jump up on the running board, and Víctor puts his hand around the back of my head, grabbing my hair and pulling me close to him, holding me tight and hugging me.

Looking past Víctor to Dad, I see that his eyes are filled with tears.

"Your mother?" Dad asks. "Your brother and sisters?"

"Mom's fine. We're all fine. Juan was sick, but he's getting better."

"Thank God," Dad says softly. Then, not really speaking to me, just saying the words out loud, he asks, "Where is the town?"

I think about Dad's words, "Where is the town?"

I know the answer, although for the moment I don't say it out loud. *We* are the pueblo. *We* are the town now.

When Dad walks into the house, Mom weeps and laughs and hits him and grabs him all at the same time. Ángela and Juan each grab and lock on to one of Dad's legs, almost toppling him over.

Mom hugs Víctor, who buries his face in her shoulder, hugging her back.

María, standing back a little, asks softly, "Where's Ruby?"

Her question hangs over the room.

"Ruby's going to be fine," Dad says. "She has a broken leg, but the doctor says that it'll mend. She's in the little clinic in Chalupe."

Dad pauses a moment, then says, "Actually, it was Víctor we were most worried about."

Víctor tries to wave off Dad's words. "It was nothing," he says. "A little bump on the head."

Dad smiles. "Yes, a 'little bump,' but he was unconscious for three days."

"I was resting," Víctor says, and then he laughs. "Actually, I don't know *what* I was doing."

We gather around the table as Dad explains what happened: "We were on the bridge when the water broke over the top. We abandoned the truck and took off running, but a huge log riding the current rammed into Ruby, breaking her leg and knocking her into the river. Víctor dove in to save her, but when he came to the surface, he was unconscious. I pulled them both to safety. God was watching over us.

"I carried them, first Víctor for a few steps, then Ruby, then Víctor again, for a mile."

He smiles. "Ruby helped by hopping on one leg. Víctor helped by not complaining. After all, he *was* unconscious."

We all laugh, and Víctor smiles.

Dad's voice sounds tired as he explains, "We went slowly. The rain was like being hit by stones, but luckily the wind was blowing from behind us, pushing us along. I can't even remember very much about the journey, just that I was so worried about Víctor and Ruby and I knew we had to make it to shelter someplace. Finally we reached Chalupe. We've been there all week, with no phones and no contact from anyone outside the town until the soldiers arrived today."

Once Dad has told his story, it's our turn. We tell
Dad and Víctor about the storm—the rains, the wind,
and the mudslide. We tell them about the doctor and
soldiers, about finding the food at the Arroyos', about
the sewer and phone and water and how I tried to go
to San Pedro Sula. But we don't tell them everything;
we don't talk yet about the dead.

We all take turns, each of us telling different parts
of the story. Mom doesn't say much. She just sits
close to Dad and keeps rubbing his arm, touching
him, and staying at his side.

Finally Juan, looking straight at Víctor, says, "José
used C-3PO, 'cause he was scared." After Juan says
this, he glances quickly at me, like these words have
slipped out by accident. He gives me a sheepish look
of apology.

Víctor smiles at Juan and says, "Oh yeah? Good. I
wish I'd had C-3PO. It was pretty scary, all right."
Juan smiles at me, and I smile back.

Sitting here with my dad and Víctor home and
knowing that Ruby is alive and safe, I feel almost like
a kid again—*almost*. I feel lighter and relaxed and
almost happy—*almost*. I'd forgotten what happiness
felt like. But even as I feel better, I know that I'm not
the same kid anymore.

As if she is reading my mind again, Berti walks across the room and lies down at my feet. I pat her head lightly, but she doesn't react at all.

"Roberta," Dad says, smiling, and he pats Berti too. "Hi, Berti," he adds, but she ignores him.

Dad smiles again and says, "Some things don't change, huh?" Suddenly he turns to me and says, "You've done a lot, José."

"Everyone has, Dad," I answer.

"Yes, I know," Dad says, "but you've had to be the man here."

Mom interrupts, "And he's done a great job." She leans over, never taking her hand off Dad's arm, and puts her other hand on my shoulder. She kisses my cheek. I manage not to blush as I wait for Víctor to tease me. If there's one thing in the world I can always count on, it's that Víctor will never let a compliment go to my head. But Víctor is quiet, and when I finally find the courage to look at him, I see that he's smiling at me too.

He says, "Very good, brother."

Now I can't stop it any longer. My face turns bright red. I say, "Everyone has done their part. Everyone."

I think about all of us digging for the dead, digging for food, sharing our water, helping each other in every way we could. I think about finding my courage again when Berti found me on the roadway. But I'll admit it: I *am* proud of what I've done.

There's a moment of silence at the table. The quiet reminds me of saying grace before dinner. I think about that word, *grace*.

God's grace.

And how graced we all are by the wild parrots that fly over La Rupa once again.

AUTHOR'S NOTE

Hurricane Mitch initially killed more than 5,000 Hondurans. In the months that followed the storm, many of the bodies of 8,000 missing people were found. Those missing who were never found are now assumed to be dead. Mitch was the worst storm in the Caribbean in two hundred years. Two hundred years! The last time Honduras had had a storm this bad, George Washington was president. Floods from Hurricane Mitch affected 70 percent of Honduras's agricultural sector. Entire villages and everyone in them were wiped out by mudslides. Hundreds of thousands of Hondurans lived for many months in shelters. Many of these shelters were in school buildings, including the school where I had taught when I lived in San Pedro Sula in 1981–82. Early estimates placed the cost of rebuilding Honduras at $3.8

billion, but the effort is still ongoing and it may take much more than that. In many of the small villages, there was no drinking water, and food supplies were dangerously low for months and even years. Dirty water became a breeding ground for mosquitoes. Malaria and dengue were rampant. People's immune systems weaken without enough food, and weak immune systems allowed these diseases to grab hold. Some people say it could take fifty years for Honduras to recover from Hurricane Mitch. Some say it will take many generations.

Like José in this story, I don't know how to respond to that kind of talk. How does one recover from the loss of everything? How does one recover from the loss of somebody, or maybe everybody, one has loved?

Although this story of José Cruz and his family is a work of fiction, and any resemblance to persons living or dead is absolutely unintentional, it is certainly based on a true event. It is my hope that by sharing this story, we may better understand that we live on a relatively small planet and that we're all family.

Terry Trueman
October 2003

ADDENDUM

In 2005, all along the Gulf Coast of the United States and especially in New Orleans, Americans learned from Hurricane Katrina what the people of Central America had learned less than a decade earlier from Hurricane Mitch. Honduras was and is a small, poor country, and perhaps in the United States we felt that nothing like Hurricane Mitch could ever happen to us. But look what a single storm was able to do to the most powerful nation on earth. This story of José Cruz and his family is fictional, but similar events have occurred over and over again in Central America since Hurricane Mitch, and in many of our tiny towns and large cities all across our Gulf Coast.

Terry Trueman
September 2006